reprints the people's bulletin

1946-1949

Foreword by Pete Seeger
Edited by Irwin Silber

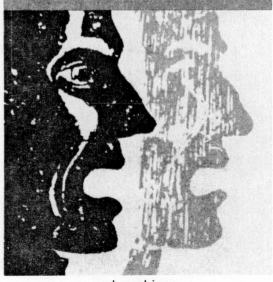

oak archives

Contents

© 1961
Oak Archives
An Imprint of The Music Sales Group
257 Park Avenue South
New York, NY 10010

By Pete Seeger

foreword

In 1945 Americans came home from the war. We dived enthusiastically into long deferred projects. A number of us who loved to sing folk songs and union songs thought it the most natural thing in the world to start an organization which could keep us all in touch with one another, which could promote new and old songs and singers, and in general bring closer the broad revival of interest in folk music and topical songs which we felt sure would sooner or later take place. We called our organization People's Songs to distinguish it from the scholarly folklore societies, and started a bulletin. I wanted it to be a weekly; others persuaded me to be more conservative and make it a monthly.

It was strictly a shoestring operation. The first issue was mimeographed. When we had to start paying a salary to at least one person ($25 a week) we felt we were being wildly extravagant. Monthly hootenannies in New York paid the office rent.

We had the utmost contempt for normal commercial musical endeavors. We were convinced that the revival of interest in folk music would come through the trade unions. After all, it was New Deal money which had sparked the great Library of Congress folk song archives in the '30's. Union educational departments had already put out many fine songbooks. There was the singing tradition of the old IWW to build on. We envisioned a singing labor movement spearheading a nationwide folksong revival, just as it was the Scottish progressives who sparked a folksong revival at the time of Robert Burns, and the Czech progressives who sparked another at the time of Dvorshak.

How our theories went astray! Most union leaders could not see any connection between music and porkchops. As the cold war deepened in '47 and '48 the split in the labor movement deepened. "Which Side Are You On" was known in Greenwich Village but not in a single miner's union local.

But here is the interesting thing: the revival of interest in folk music and topical songs did come about, and the existence of People's Songs helped to do it. How? Because the young people in summer camps and schools grew up and went to college. Because the very banishment of singers as myself from labor union work forced us to make a living in commercial ways, such as nightclubs, or in concerts for schools and colleges. Because, basically, these were good songs, as any fool could plainly see. And our theory about singing them in an informal and enthusiastic way was correct.

The organization People's Songs closed its doors for lack of funds in early 1949. We couldn't raise the (for us) huge sum of $3000 to pay printers and landlords. But the singers and songs carried on. A few years later, the magazine Sing Out started up on similar lines, and with the devoted work of a few volunteers, slowly grew. Looking over the pages of the little mimeographed bulletin of 1946 I am at times appalled by its amateurishness, and at other times filled with a flush of pride for bravery and honesty. Maybe fools walk in where angels fear to tread, but here's to the young and foolish, and may the world have more of them.

Dutchess Junction
Beacon, N.Y.
August, 1961

By Irwin Silber

introduction

Fifteen years ago, a modest little publication made its debut in the United States. Reproduced elsewhere in this book is a reproduction of the front page of Vol. 1, No. 1 of The People's Songs Bulletin.

Published monthly, The People's Songs Bulletin lasted a little over three years, expiring in the spring of 1949 of acute financial anemia. But in the course of its few short years, The Bulletin and the organization behind it, People's Songs Inc., played a most significant role in what later emerged as the folksong revival.

People's Songs was the product of its time -- and of a group of active partisans (Pete Seeger, Lee Hays, Bernie Asbel, Woody Guthrie, Waldemar Hille, Earl Robinson, Betty Sanders, Boots Casetta, Jenny Vincent, Alan Lomax, Felix Landau, Bob Claiborne, myself, and many others) who were caught up in the idealistic fervor engendered by World War II.

We believed that the world was worth saving and that we could do it with songs. We believed in the rights of labor and the brotherhood of man. We believed in the United Nations, Franklin D. Roosevelt, and the CIO. We were against Jim Crow, the atom bomb and high prices. And we were all young. Most of us were in our twenties and early thirties. Almost no one was past forty.

We also believed in folk music -- or what we understood folk music to be. We felt that we were living in the dawn of the "century of the common man" and that we were rediscovering and revitalizing the musical heritage of the common man.

We respected scholarship -- but our aims were not scholarly. We were emotionally involved with songs of the folk, and we found in these traditional airs and verses an expression for ourselves. In the folk songs of America and of other lands we found honesty, directness, righteous protest and democratic sympathy -- and images of rare and singular beauty.

In the pages of The People's Songs Bulletin we joined our political faith with our love of folk music. We called the product of this union "people's" songs -- not exactly folk music, but directly in the line of succession.

Sustained by our belief in the worth of what we were doing, we defied the basic principles of economics and somehow managed to publish our Bulletin for some three years. At the height of our achievement, we boasted some 3,000 subscribers in all the (then) 48 states. Our influence, however, could not be measured by numbers alone. For almost every reader was a song-spreader, someone who sang for others or who led songs or who utilized the songs in other ways. By-passing all the methods of mass communication, we were able to get a good new song around the country in a few weeks time, so that audiences from California to Maine would be singing "Listen Mr. Bilbo" or "Put It On The Ground" all at the same time.

Had we been "commercial," we undoubtedly would all be wealthy today, for we knew and loved and sang and rewrote almost every folk song which subsequently became a "hit" in the 1950's. In the pages of our Bulletin, without copyright claim on our part, appeared such songs as "Worried Man Blues," "Goodnight Irene" and "Tom Dooley." Our goal was world peace, not a piece of the world (with apologies to Vern Partlow) -- and the fact that we achieved neither reflected, undoubtedly, both the times we lived in and our own naivette.

In putting together this anthology, I have tried to guide myself with the following considerations:

First, I wanted to present a representative document of The People's Songs Bulletin. As you will see, almost all the material in this volume is photographically reproduced exactly as it appeared in the original. In a few cases (Pages 90 to 96) we have recopied the music because of difficulties in direct reproduction. However, in no case have we changed the actual words or music.

Second, realizing that many hard-to-come-by songs appeared among the 319 which were printed in The Bulletin, I have tried to include a good number of songs which I know people want to obtain, and to keep to a minimum the songs which are readily available elsewhere.

In addition to the songs and articles, I have put together a representative sampling of news and gossip items under the general heading of "Singing People," and I have made a culling of "Letters to the Editor" for a helping of correspondence of lasting interest.

For two years, Lee Hays wrote a monthly column for The People's Songs Bulletin, producing a collection of essays that were delightful to read, informative and provocative. One such column is included here and I hope that Lee Hays can be persuaded to let us put the rest of his columns together in book form.

The illustrations are all from the pages of The People's Songs Bulletin and I am indebted to Moses Asch for assistance in selecting and arranging the illustrative material.

I also wish to thank Daryl Heymann for assistance in preparation of the final manuscript.

To Pete Seeger, Waldemar Hille, Boots Casetta and Lee Hays, it would be presumptuous to extend thanks. This is their collection -- and mine as well.

And now it is yours.

PEOPLE'S SONGS

Bulletin of People's Songs Inc., organized to create, promote and distribute songs of labor and the American people.

Peter Seeger, Executive Secretary 130 West 42 St., N.Y., N.Y.

Vol. I. February 1946 No. 1.

> The people are on the march and must have songs to sing. Now, in 1946, the truth must reassert itself in many singing voices.
> There are thousands of unions, people's organizations, singers, and choruses who would gladly use more songs. There are many song-writers, amateur and professional, who are writing these songs.
> It is clear that there must be an organization to make and send songs of labor and the American people through the land.
> To do this job, we have formed PEOPLE'S SONGS, INC.
> We invite you to join us.

To Unions

Do you want to publish a songbook for your members? Write us for help in putting one together.

Do you want a song composed especially for your union? Would you like to have phonograph records of your own songs for use in your locals?

These are jobs which we are prepared to do. Activities directors should subscribe to this Bulletin with its regular song supplement.

To Songwriters

We are going to print the songs of both amateur and professional songwriters in this Bulletin, which goes to singers, leaders of choruses and to organizations all over the country.

Here is a new way of reaching your audience. Arrangments can be made through us to have your songs printed in sheet music form. You are assured of complete copyright and royalty protection.

Singers, Leaders of Choruses...

and performers may become members of PEOPLE'S SONGS, and receive this Bulletin. You will get many new songs you can use, and some of the older ones. If you need lyrics for other songs, we can help you find them.

"SONGS TO GROW ON"
DON'T YOU PUSH ME

By Woody Guthrie, Copyright 1947 by Woody Guthrie

Well, you can play with me, and you can hold my hand, and you can comb my hair, and you can ride my horse. You can roll my ball, and ride my trike a-round, You can ev-en laugh at me. but don't you push me down.

Chorus

DON'T YOU PUSH ME, push me, push me, don't you push me down, Don't you push me, push me, push me, Don't you push me down.

You can play with me
You can dress my doll
You can ride my scooter
And you can ride my skates,
You can take my wagon
And roll it all around,
You can even get mad at me,
But don't you push me down.
(CHORUS:)

You can play with me
We can play all day
You can use my dishes
If you'll put them away,
You can feed me apples
And oranges and plums
You can even wash my face
But don't you push me down.
(CHORUS:)

All The Pretty Little Horses

One of the most beautiful lullabies. You may know another version of it, since it's a very widespread song. Some people say that the second verse comes from the time when Negro slaves suckling their white master's babies, thought of their own children, orphaned in the slave shacks.

Hush-a - by, don't you cry, Go to sleep - y, lit - tle
When you wake you shall have, All the pret - ty lit - tle

ba - by. Blacks and Bays, Dap-ples and Grays,
hor - ses.

Coach and six - a lit - tle hor - ses. Hush - a - by,

don't you cry. Go to sleep - y , lit - tle ba - by.

Hushaby, don't you cry,
Go to sleepy, little baby.
When you wake, you shall have,
All the pretty little horses.

Way down yonder in the meadow
There's a poor little lambie;
The bees and the butterflies -
   pickin' out his eyes,
The poor little thing cried "Mammy".

(Repeat first four lines)

Hushaby, don't you cry,
Go to sleepy, little baby.
When you wake, you shall have,
All the pretty little horses.

"SONGS TO GROW ON"

SH, TA- RA- DAH- DAY

Third in our series of songs for young folks is a lullaby, a song-form we venture to say will never die out until some fiendish scientist invents an automatic mother. Carl Sandburg reports that this lullaby was learned from an Irish railroad worker in Iowa.

Mothers all over the world seem to unburden their own hearts, even though they know the kid can't understand the words; hence many lullabies are full of social comment. In the P/S library we even have union lullabies.

Many large song collections print sections of lullabies, but up to two weeks ago few of them were recorded. Two weeks ago, that is, when ye editor did a whole album full for Moe Asch of the Disc Recording Company. Others recorded besides this song: All the Pretty Little Horses, By'm Bye, Hush Little Baby Don't Say a Word, Baa Baa Blacksheep, All Night Long, Mary had a Baby, Go Tell Aunt Nancy. Anybody have a baby?

—P.S.

Shh, ta- ra-da- day, shh ta- day---. Times is might- y hard-----------. A dol-lar a day is all they pay for work on the bou----- le vard--

Another hit song from the album "Songs To Grow On" (Disc 602) composed and sung by Woody Guthrie. Let the kids go thru the motions of hammering and sawing as you sing; just watch out for the flying elbows.

"SONGS TO GROW ON"
BLING! BLANG!

By Woody Guthrie, Copyright 1947 by Woody Guthrie

You get - a ham-mer and I'll get a nail and you catch a bird and

I'll catch a snail. You bring a board and I'll bring a saw—and

we'll build a house for the ba-by- o. Bling Blang

Ham-mer with my ham-mer, Zing-o Zang-o, Cut-ting with my saw.

I'll grab some mud and you grab some clay;
So when it rains it won't wash away;
We'll build a house that'll be so strong
The winds will sing my baby a song.

Chorus: Bling. Blang.
              Hammer with my hammer.
              Zingo. Zango.
              Cutting with my saw.

              Bling. Blang.
              Hammer with my hammer.
              Zingo. Zango.
              Cutting with my saw.

Run, bring rocks and I'll bring bricks;
A nice pretty house we'll build and fix;
We'll jump inside when the cold wind blows
And kiss our pretty little babyo.

(Chorus)

You bring a ladder and I'll get a box;
Build our house out of bricks and blocks;
When the snowbird flies and the honeybee comes
We'll feed our baby on honey in the comb.

(Chorus)

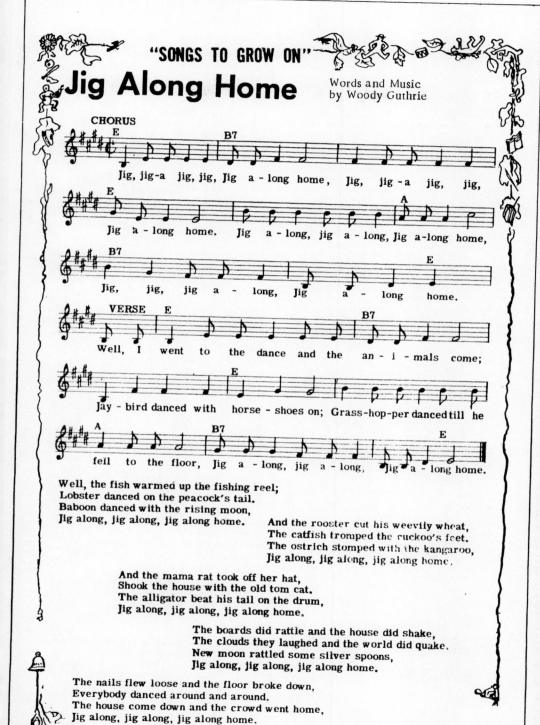

"SONGS TO GROW ON"
Jig Along Home

Words and Music
by Woody Guthrie

CHORUS

Jig, jig-a jig, jig, Jig a - long home, Jig, jig - a jig, jig,
Jig a - long home. Jig a - long, jig a - long, Jig a-long home,
Jig, jig, jig a - long, Jig a - long home.

VERSE

Well, I went to the dance and the an - i - mals come;
Jay - bird danced with horse - shoes on; Grass-hop-per danced till he
fell to the floor, Jig a - long, jig a - long, Jig a - long home.

Well, the fish warmed up the fishing reel;
Lobster danced on the peacock's tail.
Baboon danced with the rising moon,
Jig along, jig along, jig along home.

And the rooster cut his weevily wheat,
The catfish tromped the cuckoo's feet.
The ostrich stomped with the kangaroo,
Jig along, jig along, jig along home.

And the mama rat took off her hat,
Shook the house with the old tom cat.
The alligator beat his tail on the drum,
Jig along, jig along, jig along home.

The boards did rattle and the house did shake,
The clouds they laughed and the world did quake,
New moon rattled some silver spoons,
Jig along, jig along, jig along home.

The nails flew loose and the floor broke down,
Everybody danced around and around.
The house come down and the crowd went home,
Jig along, jig along, jig along home.

*orig. = kiss

Eddystone Light

English Folksong
As sung by
Richard Dyer-Bennet

A whimsical gem from the repertoire of Richard Dyer-Bennet, who picked up his songs everywhere from his native England, to Sweden where he studied under one of the 'last of the ancient bards'.

Dick Bennet, first becoming known in the US during the first years of the war, introduced an important new element to American ballad singing. Fans noted first his British accent, and his playing a fantastic looking Swedish lute; clearly this was a far cry from Leadbelly. But what was important about this new singer was his intensely professional approach, and his thorough musicianship in, for example, his guitar arrangements. Now Dick has quit the night club racket, makes a yearly concert tour, and concentrates on his 'School of American Minstrelsy' in Colorado. People's Songsters may disagree (and many do) with his particular style of singing and playing, but there is no doubt that his performer's approach to his work is one that will be adopted by many city-bred Americans who want to learn folksongs.

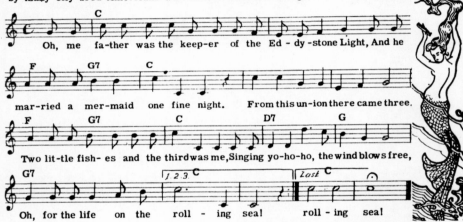

Oh, me fa-ther was the keep-er of the Ed-dy-stone Light, And he mar-ried a mer-maid one fine night. From this un-ion there came three. Two lit-tle fish-es and the third was me, Singing yo-ho-ho, the wind blows free, Oh, for the life on the roll-ing sea! roll-ing sea!

One night, as I was a-trimming of the glim,
Singing a verse from the evening hymn,
A voice on the starboard shouted "Ahoy!"
And there was my mother, a-sitting on a buoy.
(CHORUS:)

"Oh, where are the rest of my children three?"
My mother then she asked of me.
"One was exhibited as a talking fish,
The other was served from a chafing dish."
(CHORUS:)

Then the phosphorous flashed in her seaweed hair:
I looked again, and my mother wasn't there.
But her voice came echoing back from the night,
"To Hell (or "to the Devil") with the keeper of the
    Eddystone Light!" (CHORUS:)

Tom Dooley

Civil War song
As sung by Frank Warner
Used by permission

Tom Dooley is about an incident growing out of the Civil War. A returned soldier finds that things are not quite the same with his girl as they were before he left. He now has competitors for her favor. Not being able to cope with the situation, he kills the girl. The rest of the story is told in the lyrics of the song.

CHORUS G
Oh, hang down your head, Tom Dool - ey, Hang down your head and
D7
cry. Hang down your head, Tom Dool - ey, Poor boy, you're bound to
G
die.
VERSE G
I met her on the moun-tain and there I took her
D7
life. I
D7
met her on the moun-tain and stabbed her with my
G
knife.

Hand me down my banjo
I'll pick it on my knee
'Cause this time tomorrow
It'll be no use to me. (Cho.)

This time tomorrow
Where you reckon I'll be?
If it hadn't 'a-been for Grayson
I'd 'a been in Tennessee. (Cho.)

This time tomorrow
Where you reckon I'll be?
Down in some lonesome valley
A-hanging on a white oak tree. (Cho.)

Frank Warner has popularized this version of Tom Dooley. It is one of many songs which Frank will include in a book he is working on now. The release date will be announced. Some of his favorite songs can be heard in his album Hudson Valley Songs, Disc-119.

Big Rock Candy Mountain

Hobo song

There are two main versions of this perennial favorite, and we beg to be neutral in the argument that is sure to come from printing only one of them on this page. The other version has been recorded by Burl Ives and those wishing to learn it can find it in any music store. We'll not venture to say which was made up first.

One eve-ning, as the sun went down And the jun-gle fires were burn-ing, Down the track came a ho-bo, ham-ming, And he said, "Boys, I'm not turn-ing. I'm head-ed for a land that's far a-way Be-side the crys-tal foun-tains. I'll see you all this com-ing fall In the Big Rock Can-dy Moun-tains. In the Big Rock Can-dy Moun-tains There's a land that's fair and bright, Where the hand-outs grow on bush-es __ And you sleep out ev-'ry night, Where the box-cars all are emp-ty And the sun shines ev-'ry day __ Oh the birds and the bees and the cig-a-rette trees, The rock-rye springs where the whang doodle sings In the Big Rock Can-dy Moun-tains.

In the Big Rock Candy Mountains,
All the cops have wooden legs,
And the bulldogs all have rubber teeth
And the hens lay softboiled eggs.
The farmer's trees are full of fruit
And the barns are full of hay.
O I'm bound to go,
Where there ain't no snow,
Where the sleet don't fall
And the wind don't blow
In the Big Rock Candy Mountains.

In the Big Rock Candy Mountains,
You never change your socks,
And the little streams of alkyhol
Come trickling down the rocks.
The shacks all have to tip their hats

And the railroad bulls are blind,
There's a lake of stew,
And of whiskey, too,
And you can paddle all around in a big canoe
In the Big Rock Candy Mountains.

In the Big Rock Candy Mountains,
The jails are made of tin,
And you can bust right out again,
As soon as they put you in.
There ain't no shorthandled shovels
No axes, saws or picks -
I'm a-going to stay,
Where you sleep all day,
Where they boiled in oil
The inventor of toil,
In the Big Rock Candy Mountains.

Runnin', Runnin'

Negro Song
Adapted by Hally Wood

Hally Wood has taken this Negro theme and changed it a bit to suit her own singing. Keep right on 'runnin' when you perform it.

Run-nin', run-nin', run-nin', ____ I can't ___ tar-ry.

Run-nin', run-nin', run-nin', ____ I can't tar-ry.

Run-nin', run-nin', run-nin' ___ I can't ___ tar-ry.

Run-nin' up the King's high-way.

I'm weepin', Lord, I'm cryin',
I can't tarry. . . . etc.

This road is hard and rocky,
I can't tarry . . . . etc.

It's the road that leads to freedom,
I can't tarry. . . etc.

Hurry, hurry, hurry, I can't tarry.
. . . . etc.

Keep me on that road, Lord,
I can't tarry. . . . etc.

Don't let trouble stop me,
I can't tarry . . . . etc.

Runnin', runnin', runnin',
I can't tarry. . . . etc.

COLD WATER

Temperance Movement Song
As Collected by Paul Ashford

There's nothing like water to give
The strength that we need for to live
I'll go through the woods
And I'll go to the spring
And over the bubbles I merrily sing,
Cold water, cold water, cold water,
Cold water for me.

RYE WHISKEY

Frontier Ballad

On this burning issue of Demon Rum vs. Cold Water, People's Songs takes no stand, but we thought you'd like to know that songs have been sung on both sides of the question. More than a hundred years ago the American temperence movement started making up songs to try and put the drinking songs out of business. They never did quite succeed, of course, but some of the temperence songs still are wonderful fun to sing. The one on this page was learned from the Seattle folklorist, Paul Ashford, who one of these days will be publishing a book full of them.

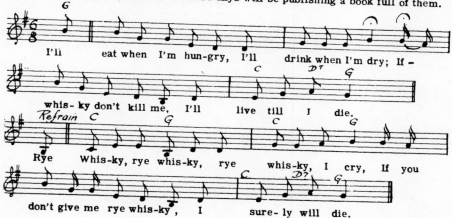

I'll eat when I'm hun-gry, I'll drink when I'm dry; If whis-ky don't kill me, I'll live till I die.

Refrain

Rye Whis-ky, rye whis-ky, rye whis-ky, I cry, If you don't give me rye whis-ky, I sure-ly will die.

I'll tune up my fiddle, and I'll rosin my bow
And make myself welcome wherever I go.
Beefsteak when I'm hungry, red liquor when I'm dry,
Greenbacks when I'm hard up, and religion when I die.
Sometimes I drink whisky, sometimes I drink rum,
Sometimes I drink brandy, at other times none.
If the ocean was whisky and I was a duck
I'd dive to the bottom and never come up.
I'll drink and I'll gamble, my money's my own,
And them that don't like me can leave me alone.
I'll buy my own whisky, I'll make my own stew;
If I get drunk, madam, it's nothing to you.
I'll eat when I'm hungry, I'll drink when I'm dry
If a tree don't fall on me, I'll live till I die.
Rye whisky, rye whisky, you're no friend to me,
You killed my poor daddy, God-damn you try me.

THE FARMER'S CURST WIFE

American Folk Song

Here's a proof of America's democratic spirit, and we'll show you why. Of all the hundreds of ballads handed down to the pioneers by their English forbears, the ones that lasted were not the 90% which were stories of kings and nobles. Instead, the four most widely sung folksongs in America which can be directly traced to British ancestry are Barbara Allen, The Dying Rake (Streets of Laredo, etc.) Black Jack Gypsy, and The Farmer's Curst Wife. The first two are stories with a moral; the third is an adventure story of a rich woman who ran off with a poor but romantic gypsy; the last is full of real 'social consciousness' satirizing the perennial war between men and women.

Of course, everyone has their own version, and so, if you like, ignore the melody printed here. But we give a number of good verses, compiled from various sources, and you can adapt them to your favorite way of singing the song.

There was an old far-mer liv'd un-der the hill, If he ain't moved a-way he's liv-in there still, Sing: Fa- di- ing- ding- fa- di- ing- ding did-dy-ing, Fa- di- ing- ding did-dy-ing, Fa- di- ing-ding did-dy- ing day.

The Devil came up to him one day
Said, "One of your family I'm going to take away."
   Oh, please don't take my eldest son,
   There's work on the farm that's got to be done.
It's all I want that wife of yours.
Well, you can have her with all of my heart.
   He picked her up upon his back
   He looked like an eagle skeered off'n the rack.
He carried her on 'bout a mile down the road.
He said, Old woman, you're a devil of a load.
   He carried her down to the gates of Hell,
   Said, Poke up the fire, boys, we'll scorch her well.
There were two little devils with ball and chain,
Up with her foot and she kicks out their brains.
   Nine little devils went climbing up the wall,
   Saying, Take her back, daddy, she'll murder us all.
So I got up next morning and spied through a crack.
I seen the old devil come a-dragging her back.
   Said, Here's your wife both sound and well
   If I'd kept her there longer, she'd 'a torn up Hell.
This only goes to show what a woman can do.
She can whup out the Devil and her husband, too.
   It shows that the women are worse than the men,
   They can go down to Hell and come back again.

TOOM-BALALAIKA

Jewish Folk Song
As Sung
By Betty Sanders

Steht a boch- er und- er tracht

Tracht und tracht die gan- ze Nacht

Wem-men zu neh- men ohn nit far schem- men

Wem-men zu neh- men ohn nit far- schem- men.

Refrain

Toom - ba- la, toom-ba- la, toom - ba- la- lai- ka.

Toom-ba- la, toom- ba- la, toom- ba- la- lai- ka.

Toom- ba- la lai- ka, spiel ba- la- lai- ka, Toom- ba- la-

lai- ka, spiel ba- la lai- ka.

Med-el, Med-el, 'chvell ba dir fre-gen
Vos ken vak-sen, vak-sen on reg-en
Vos ken bren-nen on nit oif-her-ren
Vos ken ben-ken, veh-nen on trer-ren

Nar-is-he Boch-er vos darfst du fre-gen
A stehn ken vak-sen, vak-sen on reg-en
Liebe ken bren-nen on nit oif-her-en
A hartz ken ben-ken, veh-nen on tren-nen

Notes on pronunciation:
er= as in 'air', z= ts

* * *

A prose translation of this song is as follows:

First Verse:
   A youth worries all night long about whether he can overcome his shyness enough to find himself a girl.

Second Verse:
   (The youth speaks:) "Maiden, I would ask you; what can grow without rain; what can burn without burning itself out; and what can cry without tears?"

Third Verse:
   (The maiden replies:) "Foolish boy, how can you be so stupid? A stone (implying 'nothing') can grow without rain; love can burn without burning itself out; and a heart can cry without tears".

* * *

Don't be scared away by the Jewish words here; this is one of the most charming songs we know, and the chorus is so simple any audience can join right in on it. It is in some ways the Yiddish counterpart of the song Burl Ives sings, "I Gave My Love A Cherry".

Mule Skinner's Holler

American
Folk Song

"First heard this song sung by a second cook on a ship I sailed on. He was an old Negro --must have been 65-70 years old. He sang in a high creaked voice--the most wonderful voice I ever heard in my life. And he used to tell us what the different idiomatic expressions meant. Such as: 'I'm a going to jack you soon' --I'm going to quit here soon, the line that says: 'I'm going to wash my shirt' (of course I had to clean this up a bit) meant--I'm going to start carrying a gun. The song is a real protest song, expressing the fight of the Negro people against their oppression, and the crimes committed against them (in this supposed Christian country). It is sung at log camps, and I would call it a road gang song."

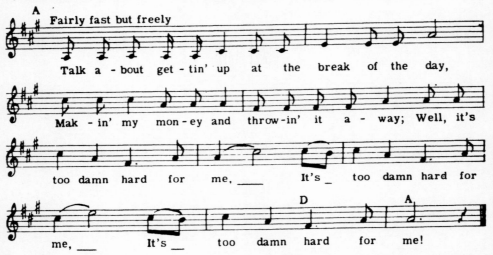

A   Fairly fast but freely

Talk a - bout get - tin' up at the break of the day,

Mak - in' my mon - ey and throw - in' it a - way; Well, it's

too damn hard for me, ___ It's ___ too damn hard for

me, ___ It's ___ too damn hard for me!

I tove Old Bet, till the break of the sweat
And it's six o'clock and it ain't day yet
And I'm gonna jack you soon,
And I'm gonna jack you soon,
And I'm gonna jack you soon.

Gonna wash my shirt and gonna starch it and sweat
And I'm gonna tell all the girls I ain't bothered yet;
And you better not bother me , ...

I heard a mighty rumblin' 'round the
watering trough
Skin a kicked the hell out of the walking boss.
Well, I ain't bothered yet . . . . .

Cisco Houston is a tall guitar picker and singer who was born in California. He has hit all the states during his 30 years of life. He sang with the migratory workers during the bad days in the West, travelling with Will Geer and Woody Guthrie, and later sang with the Almanacs. The high point of Houston's career as a singer came during the war when he shipped as a seaman. He took part in the invasion of France and other actions in the Mediterranean. In his article, he tells how singing helped the soldiers and sailors who fought and won the war.

ALL THE GUYS we used to ride on the ships with used to do some of the best singing I ever heard in my life. On one ship, the Sea Porpoise, there were a lot of Negro soldiers. We used to go down in the latrine. The acoustics there were wonderful and the singing filled the whole thing. It rang out.

And the guys from all parts of the country had wonderful stories to tell. We heard now hard it was for Negroes to get out of the South at that time, when there were good war defense jobs in Chicago and other places. They used to cut the avenues of escape. Bus lines wouldn't sell Negroes tickets just to keep them down there to work for 25¢ an hour.

These guys used to get together and sing. They had never sung together before, for they had just met on the ship. They were terrific. They had anything beat I ever heard anywhere. They didn't sing loud, just good. They chanted. All this stuff in them came out and they worked together like they had been doing it all their lives, singing. It was beautiful.

And among the soldiers and sailors and merchant marine and gun crew--the thing that brought these guys together was the singing.

At the beginning of the trip the gun crew boys were told to keep away from the merchant marine. Don't go to union meetings. Have nothing to do with the NMU. The young lieutenant who was in charge of those guys actually came down and said he didn't want the gun crew and the merchant marine together in the mess rooms, to keep them apart.

We broke that up mighty quick, by singing. After all, the gun crew boys were kids from all parts of the country. This was so much a part of their whole lives. It was ingrained in them and a little lieutenant couldn't keep them away from it.

We had all sorts of guitars and mandolins. We used to look like a walking pawnshop when we went aboard. We hauled out our instruments and got in that mess room and sang for three hours straight, Woody and Jimmy Longhi and myself and everybody else joining in. It was wonderful. We also did this down in the hold for the soldiers. They were starved for this kind of real singing. Everywhere they went, they had some corny guy from Broadway to handle the program. The soldiers didn't want to hear the kind of crap they were being offered.

But about the gun crew boys. After three nights of singing with them, even the lieutenant came down one night. After awhile he said, "Men, I'm really sorry. I never saw a bunch of guys have such a good time in all my life. I really feel bad about the way I acted. That's really the best thing I ever heard. You guys go right ahead."

Even when the ship got hit, the guys were out on the decks singing "You Fascists Bound to Lose", and singing was the thing that held them together. A lot of them were banged up, teeth knocked out, by the explosion. The phony officers were up on the deck drinking up the ship's medicinal whisky. Getting drunk to calm their nerves because they didn't know how to sing.

I saw how starved the men were for their own kind of music. Of course our stuff was something new. We sang the old songs but the good war songs that came out of the Almanacs was something they went wild about. If we'd had People's Songs Bulletins on that ship we'd have got rid of 3,000 of them-- that's how many men we had on board. These guys were landing on the beachhead. They knew that in a few hours a lot of them wouldn't be alive. Singing was the only thing that they could grab hold of.

— Cisco Houston.

The State of Arkansas

Folk song, as sung by Lee Hays

Sod Buster Ballads, & Deep Sea Chanties

In line with a general policy to re-issue outstanding albums of American folk music, Decca has put out these two albums on Commodore records—as sung by the Almanac Singers. Sod Buster Ballads contains one of the outstanding performances ever recorded of folk-style song, in the 'State of Arkansas' number.

My name is Char-lie Bren-nan, From Charles-ton I come. I trav-el'd this wide world ov-er, some ups and downs I've had, I trav-el'd this wide world ov-er some ups and downs I've saw, But I nev-er knew what mis-'ry was ____ Till I saw old Ar-kan-sas. ____

(typical variant- as in verse three)

His bread it was corn-dod-ger, His meat I could not chaw

2. I dodged behind the depot
To dodge that blizzard wind,
Met a walking skeleton
Whose name was Thomas Quin.
His hair hung down like rat tails
On his long and lathering jaw
He invited me to his hotel,
The best in Arkansas.

3. I followed my conductor
To his respected place
Where pity and starvation
Was seen on every face.
His bread it was corn-dodger
His meat I could not chaw
But he charged me a half-a-dollar
In the state of Arkansas.

SPOKEN:

Then I got me a job on a farm. But I didn't like the work, nor the food, nor the farmer, nor his wife, nor none of the children. So I went up to him one day and I told him, "Mister, I'm quitting this job, and you can just pay me off right now."

He says to me, "OK son, if that's the way you feel about it, and he handed me a mink skin." I told him, I said, "Hell, brother, I don't want this thing, I want my money."

He says to me, says: "That's what we use for currency down here in Arkansas." So I took it and headed for a saloon to see if I could get me a pint of drinking whisky. Put my mink skin on the bar, and be darned if the bartender didn't throw me a pint. Then he picked up my mink skin and h blowed the hair back on it, and he handed me three 'possum hides and fourteen rabbit skins for change. (sing again)

(Sung)
I'm going to the Indian territory
And marry me a squaw
Bid farewell to the cane-brakes
In the state of Arkansas.
If you ever see me back again
I'll extend to you my paw.
But it'll be through a telescope
From hell to Arkansas.

AIN'T IT A SHAME

American Folksong
As sung by Huddie Ledbetter

Ain't it a shame to beat your wife on Sun- day?

Ain't it a shame? ——————— Ain't it a shame-

——to beat your wife on Sun- day, Ain't it a shame?

———————— Ain't it a shame to beat your

wife on Sun- day, when you got Mon- day,

Tues- day, Wednes- day, Oh, —— Thurs- day, Fri- day,

Sat- ur- day, Ain't it a shame. ? ——————

Ain't it a shame to take a drink on Sunday
. . . (etc.)
Ain't it a shame to kiss the girls on Sunday
. . . (etc.)

24

JINNY JENKINS

Courting Song

Will you wear red, O my dear?, O my dear?
Will you wear red, Jin-ny Jen-kins? No,—
— I won't wear red, it's the col-or of my head, I'll buy me a fol-ly rol-ly dil-ly dal-ly seek-a-doub-le use a coz-zy roll to find me Roll,— Jin-ny Jen-kins, Roll.—

Will you wear green,
  O my dear, O my dear?
Will you wear green,
  Jinny Jenkins?
  O, I won't wear green
  I'm ashamed to be seen
  I'll buy me a folly rolly ..
    .. etc.

(OTHER VERSES:)
Will you wear blue- (the color's too true)
Will you wear yellow- (I'd never get a feller)
Will you wear purple- (It's the color of a turtle)
What will you wear-? (O, what do you care if I
      just go bare? . . .)

To Anacreon In Heaven

"Oh say can you see by the dawn's early light. . .''

WHILE it is well-known that this publication accepts the principle of the topical parody of an older melody, we also believe it is fair play that the earlier version also be heard in court. To that end we present some rarely heard lyrics. Here is the song which Francis Scott Key used in 1812 for his patriotic song which became our National Anthem by Act of Congress on March 3rd., 1931.

Samuel Arnold is often given credit for this tune, but the musicologist, O. G. Sonneck, in a complete and scholarly "Report on The Star-Spangl-

ed Banner," clearly proves Smith's right to be considered the composer. There are many slight variations in the melody, which has always, of necessity, been a flexible affair.

It seems that "To Anacreon In Heaven", originally the theme song of a blue-blood drinking and singing club in London, the Anacreontic Society, later became tremendously popular throughout all the colonies. True gentlemen would never sing this song in the presence of ladies.

Anacreon, of course, is the ancient Greek poet (B.C. 563-478) whose chief writings were in praise of love and wine. He is said to have died at the ripe old age of eighty-five as a result of choking on a grape seed.

Words: Ralph Tomlinson   Music: John Stafford Smith

To An - a - creon in heav'n Where he sat in full glee; A few
That __ he their in - spir - er and pa - tron would be; When this

sons of har - mo - ny sent in a pe - ti - tion.
an - swer ar - rived from the jol - ly old Gre - cian:

Voice fid - dle and flute, No __ long - er be mute, I'll

lend ye my name and in - spire ye to boot, And be -

sides I'll in - struct ye, like me, to en - twine __ The

myr - tle of Ve - nus with Bac - chus - 's vine!

Apollo rose up; and said, Pr'ythee ne'er quarrel,
Good king of the gods, with my vot'ries below!
Your thunder is useless —then, shewing his laurel,
Cried, Sic evitabile fulmen, you know!
    Then over each head
    My laurels I'll spread,
So my sons from your crackers no mischief shall dread,
Whilst snug in their club-room, they jovially twine
The myrtle of Venus with Bacchus's vine.

Little Willie

Negro Holler-Prison Song
As Sung By "Dock" Reese
Copyright 1947 By "Dock" Reese

In the fall of '46 People's Songs arranged for Dock Reese, who contributed "Little Willie", to visit New York from his home state of Texas. "Little Willie" is a work song, and was made up out of the lives of many prisoners, working all day in the hot sun. To understand it, you have to understand something of the southern prison camps, which hang over the head of any Negro who steps out of the line laid down for him by White Supremacy. Dock Reese puts it this way: "A new prisoner could not be allowed to talk while working, so he might put his story into verses of the songs they were all singing. A song might last for half an hour--these men had plenty of time." Hence all the verses. It is hard to get a real idea of the song from a piece of paper, but try and imagine a great field of cotton with three or four hundred prisoners chopping at the ground with hoes. All around stand white guards with guns, and nearby are the bloodhounds who can track down and tear to pieces anyone who tries to escape. Someone starts up a song, and without looking at each other, men join in, voices feeling out harmony, and 400 hoes move up and down in unison.

DOCK REESE

They accused me of murder,
I ain't harmed a thing,
Oh---little Willie
They said I was a forger,
I can't sign my name,
Oh my Lord.

I left my mamma
In the jail house cryin',
Oh---little Willie
"The Lord have mercy
On that boy of mine".
Oh my Lord.

Well they tell me Lousiana
Is a murderous home,
Oh---my Lord
I'll be there next summer
If not for long.
Oh my Lord

If you know you couldn't hold on,
What did you come here for?
Oh---little Willie
You oughta stayed at home
And worked on your daddy's farm,
Oh my Lord

I tell you, they have killed my partner,
Planned on murdering me,
Oh---my Lord
And putting my body
Under some live oak tree,
Oh my Lord

Mamma, if I'm not home next summer,
Don't look for me,
Oh---my Lord
I'll be dead and buried
Under the Peckerwood tree.
Oh my Lord

I've got a little girl in Austin
Keeps callin' me,
Oh---my Lord
And I'm goin' home to her
If I ever go free,
Oh my Lord

Captain, oh captain,
Won't you let me down?
Oh---my Lord
I don't believe I can make it
For another round,
Oh my Lord

Little Willie, little Willie,
Where did you come from?
Oh---my Lord
I came from Houston,
The murderous home.
Oh my Lord

One day next summer
If not for long,
Oh---my Lord
They're goin' to call my number,
And I'm goin' home,
Oh my Lord

I've got a letter from the Governor,
What do you think he said?
Oh---little Willie
Said he'd give me a pardon
If he didn't drop dead,
Oh my Lord

If I ever get lucky
And duck this blow,
Oh---my Lord
I'm goin' to spend all my time
In Buffalo,
Oh my Lord

Special Chorus

Believe I'll go to rolling,
Oh my Lord
Believe I'll go to rolling,
Oh my Lord

I wonder what's the matter,
Can't hear from home,
Oh---my Lord
I can't get no letters,
Somethin's gone all wrong,
Oh my Lord

Captain, oh captain,
Won't you let me go?
Oh---my Lord
I'll pick your cotton
And chop your row,
Oh my Lord

Greensleeves

Old English Folksong
Circa 1580

"The earliest mention of the ballad of Green Sleeves is in September 1580, when Richard Jones had licensed to him 'A New Northern Dittye of the Lady Green Sleeves'

"It has been a favorite tune from the time of Elizabeth to the present day, and is still frequently to be heard in the streets of London." -- Francis James Child, 1857

A - las, my love, ye do me wrong To cast me off dis-cur-teous-ly, And I have lov - ed you so long,__ De-light - ing in __ your com-pan - ie. Green - sleeves was all my joie, __ Green - sleeves was my de - light, Green-sleeves was my heart of gold, And who but my La - die Green - sleeves.

I bought thee kerchers to thy head
  That were wrought fine and gallantly;
I kept thee both at board and bed,
  Which cost my purse well favouredly.
(REFRAIN:)

Thy smock of gold so red,
  With pearls bedecked sumtously,
The like no other lasses had,
  And yet thou wouldest not love me.
(REFRAIN:)

Thy gown was of the grassie green,
  Thy sleeves of satten hanging by,
Which made thee be our harvest queen,
  And yet thou wouldest not love me.
(REFRAIN:)

Greensleeves, now farewel, adue!
  God I pray to prosper thee,
For I am stil thy lover true;
  Come once againe, and love me!
(REFRAIN:)

A NOTE ON THIS 16TH CENT. BALLAD

-by LOUIS UNTERMEYER

GREENSLEEVES is one of the most beautiful melodies ever written--and it is also one of the most cherished. Although it is almost four centuries old, it is timeless. Modern singers have kept it alive and have brought to us the eternal sweetness and sadness which went into its composition.

It is earlier than Shakespeare--the bard speaks of it twice in The Merry Wives of Windsor. Falstaff declaims: "Let the sky rain potatoes! Let it thunder to the tune of 'Green-Sleeves'!". The tune is also referred to when Mrs. Ford makes fun of Falstaff: "I shall think the worst of fat men. They do not more adhere and place together than the Hundredth Psalm to the tune of 'Greensleeves.'"

The song was sad in mood, but it was also employed for dancing. Moreover, although the words were originally lugubrious, they had many startling versions. Some of these versions were so suggestive that the song was known as a "wanton ditty" although we have no record of any wicked version. Parodies appeared in various anthologies, notably in A New Handful of Pleasant Delights. In one version the lover reproaches his reluctant sweetheart, reminding her how much time--and money--he has spent on her without results.

> I bought thee petticoats of the best.
> The cloth as fine as it might be;
> I gave thee jewels for thy breast,
> And all this cost I spent on thee...
> They set thee up; they took me down;
> They served thee with humility;
> Thy foot might not once touch the ground
> And yet thou would'st not love me...

The tune became so popular that it was made a religious text and "moralized to the Scripture." In the 1600's it changed its character and became the favorite tune of the battling Royalists. In the 18th century it was played with new effect in the London drawing rooms, and John Gay's Beggar's Opera gave it a mocking twist.

Today such ballad singers as Richard Dyer-Bennett, Burl Ives, Betty Sanders and Susan Reed, reanimate the song, and each gives it a fresh and distinctive interpretation.

Quantrell Side

Bexar Ballad No. 9
Collected by Frank Beddo
Copyright 1947 by Frank Beddo

COLLECTOR'S COMMENTS:

This song is from my printed collection of "Bexar Ballads" (named from Bexar County, San Antonio, Texas, where I heard most of them). The songs in this collection are unique, as I have found no counterparts or variations on them elsewhere. I also took great care to include only songs with first-class tunes and plenty of modulations. I got the "Quantrell Side" (pronounced "cantrell") from my grandmother, whose father was driven from Oklahoma (Indian Territory) in 1861 for being an Abolitionist. The song apparently refers to the western outlaw Quantrell who set up a kingdom of his own after the Civil War. The chords are rather strange, but the effect can be quite blood-freezing if it is sung right. —F.B.

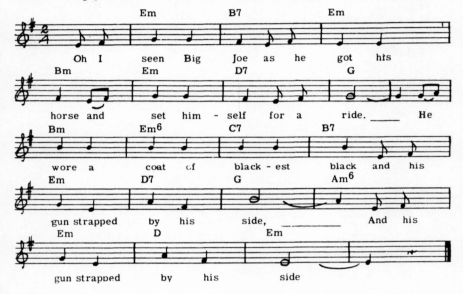

And I said, Big Joe, where do you go,
Do you go to the Quantrell side?
For the night is black and your coat
  is black,
And your gun's strapped by your side. . .

And I said, Big Joe, Oh yes I know
That they stole your sweet young bride,
But you lost your wife and you'll lose
  your life,
If you go to the Quantrell side. . .

But not a word did he say to me,
And he passed me with a stride,
And I cried, Big Joe, Oh don't you go,
Don't go to the Quantrell side. . .

Bitter Creek was bare, and they
  caught him there,
And that was the place where he died.
They killed him in his black, black coat,
With his gun strapped by his side. . .

Original Talking Blues

There have been frequent requests that we print the words of the original "Talking Blues" in the bulletin. So here they are. Ever since this traditional pattern first became generally known, many new "Talking Blues" have been written and sung -several of which are by Woody Guthrie. Some of the recent popular ones are: Talking Atomic Blues, Talking Dust-bowl Blues, Rat Hole (during the war, Woody) Talking Union, Talking Rent, Talking Bilbo Blues, and many others, even a Talking Hootenanny Blues.

American Folk Origin

If you want to get to heaven let me tell you what to do,
Got to grease your feet in a little mutton stew,
And you slide out of the devil's hand
And ooze in to the promised land.
    Take it easy, but go greasy.

Standing in the corner by the mantelpiece,
Up in the corner by a bucket of grease,
I stuck my feet in that bucket of grease,
Went a slipping up and down that mantelpiece,
    Hunting matches, Cigarette stubs, Left overs.

Down in the holler just a setting on a log,
My hand on the trigger and my eye on a hog;
I pulled that trigger and the gun went 'zip',
And I grabbed that hog with all of my grip.
    Course I cain't eat hog eyes. But I love pork chops.

Down in the hen house on my knees,
I thought I heard a chicken sneeze;
It was only a rooster saying his prayers,
And giving out thanks to the hens upstairs;
    Rooster preaching, Hen's singing. Little young pullets
        just sort of doing the best they can.

It was down behind the hen house the other night.
It was awful dark, I didn't have no light;
The farmer's dog run out by chance,
And he bit a big hole in the seat of my pants;
    I jumped a gully, Plowed ground, Rose bushes. Felt funny.

Now I'm just a City Dude a livin' out of town,
Everybody knows me as Moon-shiner Brown.
I make the beer, and I drink the slop,
Got nine little orphans that calls me Pop:
    I'm patriotic, Raisin' soldiers, Red Cross nurses.

Mama's in the front room fixing the yeast,
Daddy's in the bedroom greasing his feet;
Sister's in the back room squeezing up the hops;
Brother's at the window just a watching for the cops.
    Drinking home-brew, Getting drunk.

It Was Poor Little Jesus

Spiritual

Negro slaves were especially fond of Jesus. Though he was a white man's god, he became, through his own suffering and pain, a friend of their own. They sang about him, and their songs became shouting songs of faith in a better world than the one they knew. Songs like "It Was Poor Little Jesus" are sung today by Negro congregations, and their sympathy and tenderness still shout of a better world to come on earth. Singing about Jesus won't bring it, but it will surely help.

It was poor_ lit- tle Je - sus, Yes, yes, _____ He was born_ on ___ Christ - mas, Yes, yes, __ And _ laid_ in a man - ger, Yes, yes,___ Was-n't that a pit-y and a shame? Lord, Lord, Was-n't that a pit - y and a shame?

Poor little Jesus, Yes, yes
Child of Mary, Yes, yes
Didn't have no cradle, Yes, yes
Wasn't that a pity and a shame?
Lord, Lord
Wasn't that a pity and a shame?

Poor little Jesus, Yes, yes
They took him from a manger...
They took him from his mother...

Poor little Jesus, Yes, yes
They bound him with a halter...
And whipped him up the mountain...

Poor little Jesus, Yes, yes
They nailed him to the cross, Lord...
They hung him with a robber

Poor little Jesus, Yes, yes
He's risen from darkness...
He's ascended into glory...

He was poor little Jesus, Yes, yes
Born on Friday...
Born on Christmas

Dona nobis

3-part round
Anonymous

"Dona nobis pacem"—(give us peace)—is a round which sounds best in the original Latin. Sing it quite slowly and with sustained feeling. Anyone who has ever sung a round like 'Three Blind Mice' will know how to sing rounds. Divide your singers into groups; three, or more if the round is divided into more than three sections. The first starts singing section 1 all the way through, then, section 2, then 3, and then begins the round all over again. When the first group reaches 2, the second group starts singing 1, and so on. For practice it is good to have everybody sing the melody through in unison first.

Phonetically the words should sound 'Doh-nah noh-bees pah-chem.'

Shorty George

Prison Blues
As sung by Pete Seeger

...A prison blues, a lonesome and beautiful song. The story is that once a month a train brought the men's wives and girlfriends to visit, and at the end of the day took them away again. It was a little two-car railroad train, and they all called it "Shorty George."

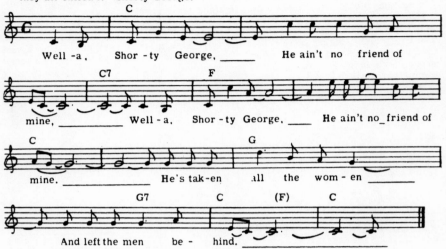

Well-a, Shor-ty George, _____ He ain't no friend of mine, _____ Well-a, Shor-ty George, ___ He ain't no_friend of mine. _____ He's tak-en all the wom-en _____ And left the men be - hind. _____

Well, my papa died, when I was just a lad (twice)
And ever since that day, I been to the bad.
Got a letter from my baby, couldn't read from crying (twice)
She said my mama weren't dead yet, but she was slowly dying.
    Well, I took my mama to the buryin' ground (twice)
    I never knowed I loved her, till the coffin sound.
Yes, I went down to the graveyard, peeped in my mam's face (twice)
"Ain't it hard to see you, in this lonesome place!"
    O, when I get back to Dallas, I'm gonna walk and tell (twice)
    That the Fort Ben' bottom is a burning Hell.

Barney Graham

Early Am. Labor Song
Words by Della Mae Graham

Of this song, Woody Guthrie has written: "Barney was killed by company guards early in 1933, during a textile strike at Davidson-Wilder, Tennessee. He was a union man 100 per cent. Now he's a union man 1000 per cent.

The governor and the State Secretary of Labor knowed of the plans to kill Barney more'n a week before the killing, but they didn't try to stop it.

This song was wrote down by Barney's daughter, Della Mae.

A time will come when Barney and Della Mae will be famous."

-- from ms. of "Hard Hitting Songs"

On A - pril the Thir - ti - eth, In Nine- teen -thir - ty three, _____ Up- on the streets of Wil - der, They shot him brave ___ and free. ____

They shot my darling father,
He fell upon the ground,
'Twas in the back they shot him,
The blood came streaming down.
    They took the pistol handles
    And beat him on the head,
    The hired gunmen beat him,
    'Till he was cold and dead.
        When he left home that morning,
        I thought he'd never return,

But for my darlin' father,
My heart shall ever yearn.
    We carried him to the grave-yard,
    And there we lay him down,
    To sleep in death for many a year,
    In the cold and sodden ground.
        Although he left the union
        He tried so hard to build,
        His blood was spilled for justice,
        And justice guides us still.

Bob L

Eating Goober Peas Civil War Song

To add a little humor to our Anniversary bulletin, here is Fred Hellerman's version of the much sung Civil War song—'Goober Peas' (peanuts today). This song was a favorite of the Confederate Army, and expresses some of the complaints the "boys in gray" had concerning the none too soft life provided by Jeff Davis.

Sit - tin' by the road - side on a sum - mer's day
Chat - tin' with my mess - mates, pass-in' time a - way,
Ly - in' in the shad-ows ___ un - der -neath the trees,
Good-ness how de - lic - cious, ___ eat - in' goob - er peas.

CHORUS

Peas, peas, peas, peas, eat - in' goob - er peas.
Good - ness how de - li - cious, ___ Eat - in' goob - er peas.

When a horseman passes the soldiers have a rule,
To cry out at their loudest. "Mister get a mule"
But still another pleasure enchantinger than these.
Is wearing out your molars, eating goober peas. (CHORUS)

Just before the battle the gen'ral hears a row,
He says, "The Yanks are coming. I can hear their rifles now."
He turns around in wonder, and what do you think he sees?
The Georgia Militia, eating goober peas. (CHORUS)

I think my song has lasted almost long enough,
The subject's interesting, but the rhymes are mighty rough;
I wish the war was over, when free from rags and fleas,
We'd kiss our wives and sweethearts, and gobble goober peas.
(CHORUS)

Times Gettin' Hard

New words by Lee Hays
American Folksong

The original of this is in what Woody Guthrie called Carl Songburg's Sandbag. In the Almanac days I used to sing it for the sake of its very pretty melody, but I hummed some of the lines to avoid words which I did not like. One day, for the sake of having some decent words to sing I wrote these extra verses. Pete Seeger and I sang it once or twice and filed it in the Almanac files where it has remained all these years. Pete remembered it and we searched for it again this month. It is a true case of a genuine folk song, and I know it is genuine because I wrote it.   -- Lee Hays --

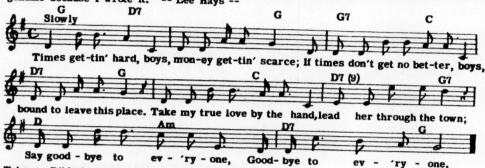

Times get-tin' hard, boys, mon-ey get-tin' scarce; If times don't get no bet-ter, boys, bound to leave this place. Take my true love by the hand, lead her through the town; Say good - bye to ev - 'ry - one, Good- bye to ev - 'ry - one.

Take my Bible from the bed, shotgun from the wall,
Take old Sal and hitch her up, the wagon for to haul;
Pile the chairs and beds up high, let nothing drag the ground--
Sal can pull and we can push--we're bound to leave this town.

Made a crop a year ago, it withered to the ground;
Tried to get some credit but the banker turned me down.
Goin' to Californ-i-ay where everything is green,
Goin' to have the best farm you ever have seen.

Times gettin' hard, boys, money's gettin' scarce.
Times has got no better, boys, goin' to leave this place.
Take my true love by the hand, lead her through the town--
Say goodbye to everyone, goodbye to everyone.

Lee Hays

As teacher of dramatics at Commonwealth, I had to think up a show for my students to do every Saturday night, when the neighbors were invited. A lot of the kids were from New York and the East, and naturally they inclined toward plays like "Waiting For Lefty" and "Private Hicks"--exactly the wrong kind of stuff for west Arkansas hill farmers, who didn't know about New York taxi drivers, didn't care about them, and thought plays about them to be in the worst possible taste.

Once in a while we'd get Mrs. Dusenberry over and build a show around her. Attendance always increased on those nights. The Easterners didn't think much of Mrs. Dusenberry's high, cracked, rhythmless voice, and made no bones about their displeasure. But they had to admit that the neighbors did come to hear Mrs. Dusenberry, and that was one of the prime objects of the drama class.

Staging Mrs. Dusenberry was easy. Sitting in an old fashioned rocking chair downstage, her blind eyes peering over the footlights, leaning forward, she looked for all the world like the Epstein statue of Gertrude Stein. And behind her, to the left, we placed Ory Dusenberry on a low chair. Ory would never remove her sun bonnet; said the spotlights would surely blister her if she did. The two of them made a nice picture.

People cherished the old lady. She was part of their history. She told the young farmers about the covered wagon days, about plowing with wooden plows behind oxen or, in bad times, cows. She told the young girls how to spin and how to make counterpanes for their wedding beds.

But they were poor, and when Mrs. Dusenberry was in her greatest need they could do little for her. Once in a while the farmers would go to the relief office and bring a load of provisions for her, but that was all. She had to stretch her twelve dollar blind check through the month when it came.

It developed that Mrs. Dusenberry was a distant cousin of mine. Anyhow, she named several of my kinfolk and told me she was a seventh cousin. She was a Hayes, she said. "There's no 'e' in my name," I told her. "Oh," she said, "one of your grandfathers dropped the 'e' out of his name as a disguise. He was a farmer in North Carolina, and he and a Negro slave woman killed his wife and salted her down in a barrel. Then they took a covered wagon and moved to Arkansas, using the contents of the barrel for provender, and dropping the 'e' as a disguise." And that, Mrs. Dusenberry told me, was how my branch of the family got started.

Late one night in October Ory came to my house on the campus and woke me. Some ruffians, she said, were plaguing her, driving up and down the road and shouting obscenities at her. Would I please lend her my gun so she could defend herself?

I got a fellow teacher out of bed and we drove Ory home. We sent her into the house and we sat on the porch, revolvers and shotguns in our laps, all that cold night. But no cars went by. It seems to me now that Ory enjoyed herself with that little dream. Thinking back on it, I don't know who in that neighborhood would have singled Ory out for their attentions. That was the only time Ory ever asked anything for herself. The rest of the time she sat behind her mother, prompting her, carding wool, quiet and obscure. With all the attention the old lady got, I think she just wanted a little, too.

Folklorists like to talk about the pure Elizabethan speech and song of the mountain people of the Southeast. I have never heard anything that I would consider pure Elizabethan speech or song. Maybe it's so. I've never met a specimen of a hill person who was as quaint and isolated as folklorists say. In fact, I knew an old mountaineer who made a fine game out of manufacturing folklore for visiting collectors. I sat on the end of his porch one day and heard him make up one tale after another about dogs. The lady collector had said, "Now, Mr. Benner, can you give me anything on dogs?" "Yes ma'am," he said, "I can give you dern near anything you want on dogs." And he sat there for three quarters of an hour making up dog stories. In fact, he told the lady more about the ways of dogs than she knew he was telling her. And the stories appeared, duly analyzed with comparative notes, in the lady's folklore thesis for a North Carolina college degree.

Anyhow, one of these folklore persons had made the mistake of telling Mrs. Dusenberry that she was Elizabethan. The old lady never got over it. She would introduce a song by saying, "I know a little Elizabethan song, made up by a man in Georgia."

Stir the pudding, Peggy,
And give those ducks a turn;
Be quick, be quick,
You lazy girl,
Or one or both will burn.

The "Jealous-Hearted Husband" told of a man who came home to find his wife had callers.

I called on my dear loving wife,
Kind sir, she answered me,
What's this hat a-doing in the hall
Where my hat ought to be?

You old fool, you blind fool,
Can't you very well see?
'Tis only a sewing bag
My mammy sent to me.

She sang of the house in Baltimore, sixteen stories high, with every room in that house filled with chicken pie.

The old lady claimed she knew 500 songs, and various collectors had recorded several hundred. Some of these came into the Almanac repertory, and some have been reprinted in the bulletin. Waldemar Hille recorded her. Hille bought her a cow, which she said was more than the other collectors had done for her, though they were long on promises.

Well, Emma Dusenberry is dead and gone, God rest her. I had the honor of singing one of her songs at Carnegie Hall once...her songs are good enough to be sung everywhere.

STIR THE PUDDING

American Folk Song
As Sung By Emma Dusenberry
Collected by W. Hille

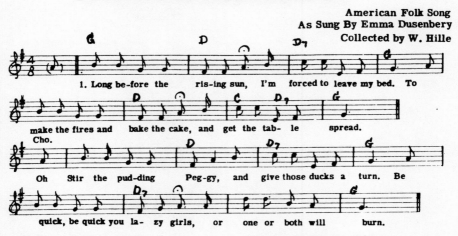

1. Long be-fore the ris-ing sun, I'm forced to leave my bed. To make the fires and bake the cake, and get the tab-le spread.

Cho.
Oh Stir the pud-ding Peg-gy, and give those ducks a turn. Be quick, be quick you la-zy girls, or one or both will burn.

Here I come beside the fire
A-turning 'round and 'round;
I hear the kipfel a-boiling,
I hate the very sound. (CHORUS)

Oh, rock the cradle, Susie,
Oh, rock the cradle on;
Oh, rock the cradle, Susie,
And keep the baby warm. (CHORUS)

The twelve days of Christmas

Last year at this time we published such songs as "Go Where I Send Thee", "Walk in Peace", "Jesus Christ was a Man" and "Free and Equal Blues". Here are a few more favorites for your use during the Xmas holidays. We hope you will still be able to sing them when the bulletin arrives.

Old English

1. On the first day of Christ-mas my true love sent to me

par-tridge in a pear tree. 2. On the sec-ond day of Christ-mas my

true love sent to me Two tur-tle doves_ and a par-tridge in a pear

tree. 3. On the third day of Christ-mas my true love sent to me
4. On the fourth (etc)

(3) Three French hens, Two tur-tle doves and a par-tridge in a pear
(4) Four col-ly birds, (etc.)

tree. (5) Five gol-den rings, Four col-ly birds,

Three French hens, Two tur-tle doves And a par-tridge in a pear

tree.

(6) Six geese a - lay - ing,
(7) Seven swans a-swimming,
(8) Eight maids a-milking,
(9) Nine drummers drumming,
(10) Ten pip-ers piping,
(11) Eleven ladies dancing,
(12) Twelve lords a-leaping,

* A__B Repeat this measure as often as necessary to get the
verses in from 6 to 12. The text should be sung accumulatively
in reverse order, using the varient which comes with No. 5 -
"Five Golden Rings"- for all verses after 5. -until the end.

Cherry Tree Carol

Did you know that Jesus was born on
January 6th? Many southerners believe it, at
any rate, and celebrate "Old Christmas".
They take their reckoning from facts: The
Julian calendar places Christmas on that
date, and it is a sworn truth that cows are
in the habit of kneeling down at midnight of
January 6th and moaning soft prayers to
celebrate Christ's birth. For those mountain families who live under Old Christmas,
the Cherry Tree Carol is standard equipment, and to go against the facts is to go
against all reason.

When Jo - seph was an old man, An old man was_
he, He _ mar-ried Vir-gin Ma-ry The_ queen of Gal-li-
lee. He mar-ried Vir-gin Ma-ry The_ Queen of Gal-li-lee.

Then Mary spoke to Joseph so meek
   and so mild,
"Joseph, gather me some cherries,
   for I am with child."

Then Joseph grew in anger, in anger
   grew he:
"Let the father of thy baby gather
   cherries for thee."

Then Jesus spoke a few words, a few
   words spoke he:
"Let my mother have some cherries,
   bow low down, cherry tree!"

The cherry tree bowed low down, bowed
   low down to the ground,
And Mary gathered cherries while
   Joseph stood around.

The Poor Mans' Family

Irish-American strike ballad. Cop.1948 Camp Woodland

Of the many indigenous strike songs made up during the early years of the American labor movement, this song must have at one time been very popular, since it has been uncovered by folklorists in several widely separated localities. The exact strike which inspired this song probably was on the New York waterfront during the 1880's or 90's. The fourth verse refers to the common employer technique, not only of those days but of much more recent times, of importing large numbers of some other racial or national minority to break the strike, setting worker against worker and diverting public attention from the real problem.

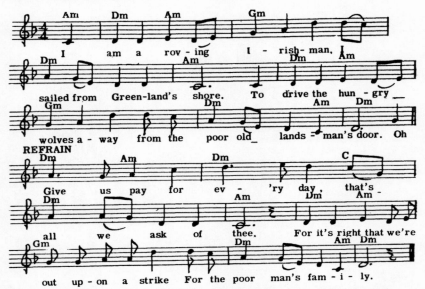

I am a rov-ing I-rish-man. I sailed from Green-land's shore. To drive the hun-gry wolves a-way from the poor old lands = man's door. Oh

REFRAIN

Give us pay for ev-'ry day, that's all we ask of thee. For it's right that we're out up-on a strike For the poor man's fam-i-ly.

The rich man's home by the cheery fire,
And their horses swift and strong:
If a poor man should ask for a crust,
They'd tell him that he's wrong.
(REFRAIN:)

"You take your ribbons in your hand
And you go and plow for me,
You can die or live,I'll have nothing to give
For the poor man's family! '' (REFRAIN)
(REFRAIN:)

They'll bring their Italians over here,
And the Negroes from the South,
Thinking they can do our work,
Take the bread from a poor man's mouth.
(REFRAIN:)

And the American children,
   they must starve?
And that we'll not agree:
To be put down like a worm in the ground,
For to starve a family (REFRAIN)

George Edwards

CATSKILL FESTIVAL

This summer marks the 10th anniversary of the Catskill Mountain Festival, which was started by Norman Studer, of Camp Woodland. Ten years ago they were told, "Of course, you know there aren't any real folksongs left up here in the mountains. We've been living here for years and never heard a single old ballad". The person who told them this, however, has seen his words disproved every year since then.

100 years ago, the thriving logging industry in the Catskills brought forth a rich tradition of popular singing. Irish raftsmen took logs to Philadelphia and in the 1840's also, the early unions came to the support of the upstate farmers who were striking against the high rents demanded by the powerful upstate landlords. At that time, the farmers even started a political movement called agrarianism, and in those days, if you called a man an agrarian it was like calling him a red. Later on, these rebellious farmers became the basis of the Free Soil and Republican parties. Songs reflected all of this activity.

In the summer of '47, George Edwards, native octogenarian, took a group of Woodland campers and counsellors down on the Delaware River to visit a distant relative of his. He was one Charles Hinkley, a woodchopper, who not only knew many old tunes, but made up new ones, about his neighbors, his home town and local events. Along around the end of a long song-swapping session, Mr. Hinkley came forth with "Poor Man's Family", which he said he had learned from his father.

A young Vassar musicologist, Norman Cazden, transcribed the melody, and is the main archivist for the Festival. By now he has collected 150 songs and tunes which he hopes to publish shortly. Each festival is composed of three parts: old folksongs of the Catskills; the campers singing songs they have learned; and compositions by serious composers based upon Catskill Mountain themes.

The composition of three years ago, a cantata by Herbert Hautrecht, "We Come From The City", has just been published by Leeds Music, and they are already receiving enthusiastic letters from various other camps which have performed it.

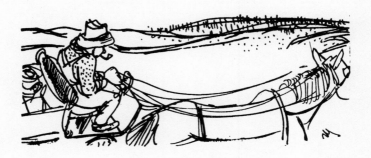

The Fireship

Sea Shanty

'The Fireship' is an old english sea shanty of the 'forecastle' variety. This would signify that it was sung when the days work was over. This version is as sung by Betty Sanders, NY People's Artist, and is from the growing collection which may become known as "Betty's Bawdy Ballads."

As I walked out one eve-en-ing up-on my night's car-reer I spied a pret-ty fire-ship and to her I did steer, I hoist-ed up my sig-an-al which she did quick-ly view, __ And when I had my bunt-ing úp, She im-med'ate-ly hove to _____ She had a dark and rov-ing eye _____ And her hair hung down in ring-e-lets, ___ A nice girl, a de-cent girl, but One of the rak-ish kind.

Excuse me, sir, she said to me
For being out so late
For if my parents knew of this
Then sad would be my fate
My father was a minister
A good and virtuous man
My mother is a Methodist
I do the best I can . . .

I took her to a tav-er-in
And treated her with wine
O little did I ever think
That she was of the rakish kind
I handled her, I dandled her
But much to my surprise
She was only an old pirate ship
Rigged up in a disguise . . .

So listen all you sailormen
Who sail upon the sea
Beware of them there fire ships
One was the ruin of me
Beware of them, stay clear of them
They'll be the death of you
T'was there I had my mizzen sprung
And my strong-box broken through . . .

The Gol-Dern Red

Boston Tea Tax Song

Early American
Ballad
As sung by
John Allison

Seeing as this is the third Fourth of July which the infant People's Songs has observed, it is about time we published one of the best of all songs of America's Revolutionary War. For more like it, we suggest you look up "Early American Ballads", sung by John and Lucy Allison,

And t'other day the Yankee folks
  Were mad about the taxes,
And so we went like Injuns dressed
  To split tea chests with axes.
It was the year of Seventy-three,
  And we felt really gritty.
The Mayor he would have led the gang,
  But Boston warn't a city! . . .

You see we Yankees didn't care
  A pin for wealth or booty,
And so in State street we agreed
  We'd never pay the duty;
That is, in State street 'twould have been,
  But 'twas King street they call'd it then,
And tax on tea, it was so bad,
  The women wouldn't scald it then. . .

To Charleston Bridge we all went down
　　To see the thing corrected;
That is, we would have gone there,
　　But the bridge it warn't erected.
The tea perhaps was very good,
　　Bohea, Souchong, or Hyson,
But drinking tea it warn't the rage,
　　The duty made it poison. . .

And then aboard the ships we went
　　Our vengeance to administer,
And we didn't care one tarnal bit
　　For any king or minister.
We made a plaguey mess of tea
　　In one of the biggest dishes;
I mean we steeped it in the sea
　　And treated all the fishes. . .

And then you see we were all found out,
　　A thing we hadn't dreaded.
The leaders were to London sent
　　And instantly beheaded;
That is, I mean they would have been
　　If ever they'd been taken.
But the leaders they were never cotch'd,
　　And so they saved their bacon. . .

Now heaven bless the president
　　And all this goodly nation,
And doubly bless our Boston Mayor
　　And all the corporation;
And may all those who are our foes,
　　Or at our praise have falter'd,
Soon have a change--that is, I mean
　　May all of them get halter'd. . .

We wish you a Merry Christmas

Christmas Carol
Anonymous

We wish you a Mer-ry Christ-mas, We wish you a Mer-ry

Christ-mas, We wish you a Mer-ry Christ-mas and a Hap-py New Year.

The Buffalo Skinners

Cowboy song
Collected by
John Lomax

We always like to point out this song to folksingers of the "purist" kind who claim they would sing "the nice old ballads but not these modern propaganda songs". We suspect that they don't realize that half the best old songs were red hot propaganda in their day. How many people today who sing "John Brown's Body" think of the way that great old fighter was reviled by America's most respectable citizens years ago? And take this "Buffalo Skinners", one of the finest of all cowboy songs: first, the singer admits to a state of unemployment (don't mention the word); then he insists upon free transportation (portal-to-portal pay, no less!); he complains of working conditions, and then when the boss reneges on pay, he kills him (the Un-American Committee would have us all in the pokey for writing such a song like this now, we're positive).

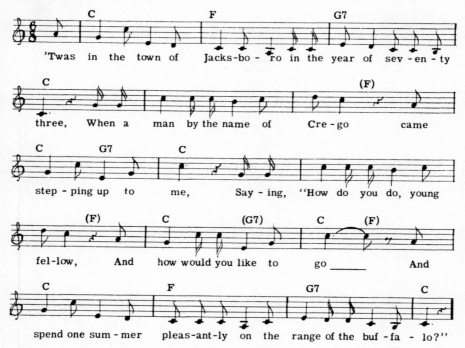

'Twas in the town of Jacks-bo-ro in the year of sev-en-ty three, When a man by the name of Cre-go came step-ping up to me, Say-ing, "How do you do, young fel-low, And how would you like to go _____ And spend one sum-mer pleas-ant-ly on the range of the buf-fa-lo?"

It's me being out of employment, boys, to old Crego I did say,
"This going out on the buffalo range depends upon the pay.
But if you will pay good wages, give transportation, too,
I think, sir, I will go with you to the range of the buffalo."

It's now we've crossed Pease River, our troubles have begun,
The first damned tail I went to rip, it's how I cut my thumb!
The water was salty as hell-fire, the beef I could not go,
And the Indians waited to pick us off, while skinning the buffalo.

The season being near over, boys, old Crego, he did say
The crowd had been extravagant, was in debt to him that day.
We coaxed him and we begged him, but still it was no go -
So we left his damned old bones to bleach on the range of the buffalo.

Oh, it's now we've crossed Pease River and homeward we are bound,
No more in that hell-fired country shall ever we be found.
Go home to our wives and sweethearts, tell others not to go,
For God's forsaken the buffalo range and the damned old buffalo.

From the painting "PONY EXPRESS" by Frank Mechau

Fair & Free Elections

Early American

This song appeared during the period of the Alien and Sedition Laws (Circa 1795), when the government was attempting to intimidate voters. It deserves to be sung today.

While some on rights and some on wrongs
Prefer their own reflections,
The people's rights demand our song –
The right of free elections.

For government and order's sake
And laws important sections,
Let all stand by the ballot box
For freedom of elections.

REFRAIN:

Law and order be the stake
With freedom and protection.
Let all stand by the ballot box
For fair and free elections.

Each town and county's wealth and peace,
Its trade and all connections.
With science, arts must all increase
By fair and free elections.

Then thwart the schemes of fighting lands
And traitor disaffections.
Stand up with willing hearts and hands
For fair and free elections.
REFRAIN:

Should enemies beset us round
Of foreign fierce complexions.
Undaunted we can stand our ground
Upheld by free elections.

Elections are to make us laws,
For trade, peace and protection.
Who fails to vote forsakes the cause
Of fair and free elections.
REFRAIN:

New York City

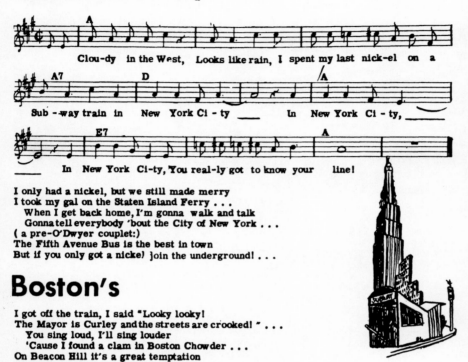

Clou-dy in the West, Looks like rain, I spent my last nick-el on a
Sub-way train in New York Ci-ty ___ In New York Ci-ty, ___
___ In New York Ci-ty, You real-ly got to know your line!

I only had a nickel, but we still made merry
I took my gal on the Staten Island Ferry . . .
  When I get back home, I'm gonna walk and talk
  Gonna tell everybody 'bout the City of New York . . .
(a pre-O'Dwyer couplet:)
The Fifth Avenue Bus is the best in town
But if you only got a nickel join the underground! . . .

Boston's

I got off the train, I said "Looky looky!
The Mayor is Curley and the streets are crooked! " . . .
  You sing loud, I'll sing louder
  'Cause I found a clam in Boston Chowder . . .
On Beacon Hill it's a great temptation
To waste your life in conversation . . .

Chicago Version

When I looped the loop, I rocked and reeled
I thought the Cubs played in Marshall Field -
(CHO:) In the Windy City, in the Windy City
  In the Windy City, blowin' all the time.
The Wrigley tower goes to kingdom come -
Fifty stories of chewing gum . . .
  There's another building across the Square
  McCormick built it out of just hot air . . .
He don't get credit, ain't it a pity?
He's the big wind in the Windy City . . .

Santa Claus Blues

Have you ever heard a Christmas carol played by a boogie-woogie pianist? We have, and thought it very sincere, moving and proper. "Each poet must sing in his own voice." And now comes another wonder - a Christmas blues. Made of verses from blues, it was introduced at the Village Vanguard by Hallie Wood. Well, can't a person feel blue at Christmas time?

(Refrain)

San-ta Claus, San-ta Claus lis-ten to my plea. San-ta

Claus, San-ta Claus, San-ta Claus - lis-ten to my plea. I don't want

noth-in' for Christ-mas, but my ba-by back to me. (Fine)

Good morn-in' blues. Blues, how do you do? Good morn'-in'

blues. Blues, how do you do? Well, I

feel al-right, But I've come to wor-ry you. Well, to-

mor-row's Christ-mas, And I want to see San-ta Claus; Well, to-

mor-row's Christmas time, And I want to see San-ta Claus. I don't get my

ba-by for Christ-mas I'll break all the laws! (D.C. al fine)

53

CHANGES

GEE BUT I DO WANT A HOME
To the tune of a well known Army song,
"Gee, But I Want To Go Home"

By Bob & Adrienne Claiborne, Harry And
Renee Berlow, And Gladys Bashkin -1947

The house I used to live in
They said was mighty fine
The ceiling tumbled in one day
And killed a pal of mine
   I'm sick of looking for a place to live
   Gee but I DO want a home

The homes they're gonna build us
They say are mighty fine
They make them out of double talk
Instead of yellow pine. ....

Harry down in Washington
And Thomas (Dewey) in New York
They seem to think that houses
Are brought here by the stork ....

Our congressmen are scheming
To take the lid off rent
It seems they want to see us all
Start living in a tent ....

So listen all you people
To what we have to say
Just fight that housing shortage
The good old Union way ....

Join the Picket Line Today

Words: Anthony-Trembke
Tune:"Alexander's Ragtime
Band"

Come on along, come on along,
Join the picket line today.
Come on along, come on along,
Join the strike for higher pay.
  And if the scabs try to break
  us
  Here's what we'll say,
  "Shame on you, scab,
  Did you work hard today?
We'll win a raise the union way,
In spite of you."
Come on along, come on along,
Join the picket line today
Come on along, come on along,
Join the strike for higher pay.

And when the boss is sure
He's got us licked,
We'll still be singing,
Come on along, come on along,
Join the picket line today!

One of the most famous examples of lyric changes is what Paul Robeson has for many years done with "Old Man River". In the bridge, instead of the word "drunk", he sings, "show a little spunk and you land in jail". And he then finishes the song, "But I keeps laughing, instead of crying; we must keep fighting until we're dying; and old man river, he just keeps etc." Has had many an audience on its feet, cheering.

✬ ✬ ✬

The verses to "Boston City" remind us of the verse tacked on to "Acres Of Clams" by Tom Glazer, Jenny Wells, and others at one of Boston's first and best hoots. It's nothing more or less than the famous verse:

Here's to the City of Boston
The land of the bean and the cod
Where the Lowells speak only to Cabots
And the Cabots speak only to God.
    And the Cabots speak only.....etc.
                  By J. C. Bossidy
Try it yourself; fits the tune perfectly!

Denver is not to be outdone by Boston, to the tune of Acres of Clams:
  Here is to the City of Denver
  The City of silver and gold
  Where the old folks come to get younger
  And the young folks never get old.

"OLD MA BELL"

Telephone strikers on the picket-lines last month all over the nation produced some parodies of their own to make the hours fly faster while they were marching up and down. A Chicago people's songster sang at one of their strike meetings and noted these verses, which they had put to "Hinky Dinky Parley-voo":
"Old Ma Bell can go to hell (3 times)
And somebody else can ring the bell
Hinky-dinky parley-voo.
The cops are standing against the wall
They're afraid the damned old building will fall, etc.
The cops don't know what it's all about,
They're letting the scabs go in and out, etc."

"TALKING RENT"

If folks in your neighborhood are threatened with evictions in the next few months you might pull out your guitar and sing them "Talking Rent" by Harry Berlow. It starts off,

If you want to keep your rent down
    Let me tell you what to do,
You got to talk to all the neighbors
    In the house with you....

and later on, the prize stanza:

Now, a landlord figures things
    Kinda funny;
Wants to raise your rent so he can
    Use your money
To buy a big car....a brand new yacht;
He wouldn't care if you didn't have
    a pot....
    ....To cook in.

VARIETY reports on a 'jingle that jangles', written by a radio man selling the Marshall Plan to Europeans.

Marshall Plan hits the spot,
Five million dollars, that's a lot;
Twice as much as the Russians too,
Marshall Plan is the Plan for you!

Who has recently been singing 'When the Saints Go Marching In'''? A standby for hot jazz fans as well as folk music lovers, it's seen many improvised verses. Claude Williams says his union members in Tennessee used these:

"O when the New World is revealed
O when the New World is revealed
Lord, I want to be in that number,
When the New World is revealed.

When the south is organized . . . etc.

When the union marches in . . . etc.

What other verses have readers used?

A union singer proposes a small change in the old labor song 'Solidarity Forever' to suit the temper of the times, For: "When the union's inspiration thru the workers' blood shall run", sing: "When the workers' inspiration thru the unions' blood shall run".

From Detroit Barbara Cahn writes that auto workers are singing new words to an old lullabye:

"Go tell young Henry,
Go tell young Henry,
Go tell young Henry,
The Old Ford system's dead."

--Drawn for People's Songs by William Steig

Roll On, Columbia

Words
and
Music
By Woody Guthrie

In 1941 Woody Guthrie travelled through the northwest territory, and made up some 19 songs which were taken down on acetate records by the Bonneville Power Administration. In 1946 Mike Loring was hired as director of information by Bonneville, and found these songs had hardly ever been used. Even the DISC album in which Woody had later recorded commercially some of the songs, was little known in Portland. So Mike started singing them on his radio programs, in the night club where he worked, and now "Roll on, Columbia" is even being included in Portland school books. Mike writes, "It's amazing how Woody got exact historical details and color in the short time he was here."

Green Doug - las Fir where the wa - ters cut through, ___ Down her wild moun-tains and can - yons she flew, Can - a - dian North-west to the O - cean so blue, It's roll on, Co - lum - bia, Roll on! ___

CHORUS
Roll on, ___ Co - lum - bia, roll on! Roll on, ___ Co - lum - bia, roll on! Your Pow - er is turn - ing our Dark-ness to Dawn; (so,) Roll on, Co - lum - bia, Roll on! _____

Other great rivers add power to you,
Yakima, Snake, and the Klickitat, too,
Sandy Williamette, and Hood river, too;
Roll on, Columbia, roll on! . . .

It's there on your banks that we
    fought many a fight.
Sheridan's boys in the block house that night,
They saw us in death, but never in flight,
Roll on, Columbia, roll on! . . .

Our loved ones we lost there at Coe's
    little store,
By fireball and rifle, a dozen or more,
We won by the Mary and soldiers she bore;
Roll on, Columbia, roll on! . . .

Remember the trial when the battle was won
The wild Indian warriors to the tall
    timber run,
We hung every Indian with smoke in his gun;
Roll on, Columbia, roll on! . .

Year after year we had tedious trials,
Fighting the rapids at Cascades and Dallas,
The Injuns rest peaceful on Menaloose Isle,
Roll on, Columbia, roll on! . . .

At Bonneville now there are ships in
    the locks,
The waters have risen and cleared all
    the rocks,

Ship loads of plenty will steam past
the ducks, so,
Roll on, Columbia, roll on! . . .

And on up the river is Grand Coulee Dam,
The mightiest thing ever built by a man, -
To run the great factories and water
the land, It's
Roll on, Columbia, roll on! . . .

These mighty men labored by day and
by night
Matching their strength 'gainst the river's
wild flight,
Through rapids and falls they won the
hard fight,
Roll on, Columbia, roll on! . . .

Mike Loring sings verses 1,2, then adds
this one, concluding with the last two.

Tom Jefferson's vision would not let
him rest -
An empire he saw in the Pacific
Northwest!
Sent Lewis and Clark and they did
the rest, so,
Roll on, Columbia, roll on! . . .

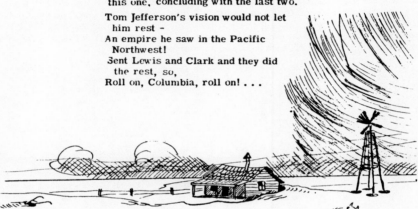

The Praties
Irish "Potato Famine" song
Dates to 19th Cen. immigration to U.S.

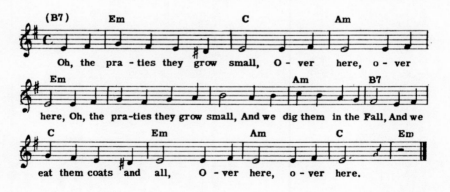

Oh, the pra-ties they grow small, O-ver here, o-ver
here, Oh, the pra-ties they grow small, And we dig them in the Fall, And we
eat them coats and all, O-ver here, o-ver here.

Oh I wish that we were geese,
Night and morn, night and morn,
Oh I wish that we were geese,
For they fly and take their ease,
And they live and die in peace,
Eatin' corn, eatin' corn.

Oh we're trampled in the dust,
Over here, over here,
Oh we're trampled in the dust,
But the Lord in whom we trust
Will give us crumb for crust,
Over here, over here.

(Repeat the first verse softly)

The Preacher And The Slave

Music To An Old Gospel Hymn
Words By Joe Hill
Used By Permission Of The I.W.W.

Better known as "Pie In The Sky", this song is best understood in the light of the times in which it was first sung. It seemed as though all that was "respectable" in America was opposed to the One Big Union idea. In addition to the bankers and the conservative newspapers, reactionary preachers carried the war into their pulpits, and the Wobblies fought back the best way they could.

If a Salvation Army band stood on one corner singing about subservience on earth and reward in heaven, the Wobblies would be likely to start a rival street singing on the opposite corner, singing their own words to the same hymn tunes. And this is one of them.

1. Long-haired preach-ers come out ev-'ry night; Try to tell you what's wrong and what's right; But when asked a-bout some-thing to eat, They will an-swer with voic-es so sweet:

Refrain

You will eat by and by you will eat by by and by In that glo-ri-ous land a-bove the sky. 'way up high Work and pray; work and pray live on hay; live on hay You'll get pie in the sky when you die. That's a lie!

If you fight hard for children and wife,
Try to get something good in this life
You're a sinner and bad man, they tell;
When you die you will sure go to hell.

Holy Rollers and jumpers come out,
And they holler, they jump and they shout.
"Give your money to Jesus", they say,
"He will cure all diseases today."

And the starvation army they play,
And they sing and they clap and they pray.
Till they get all your coin on the drum,
Then they'll tell you when you're on the bum:

Workingmen of all countries, unite.
Side by side we for freedom will fight
When the world and its wealth we have gained
To the grafters we'll sing this refrain:

Final REFRAIN: You will eat, by and by,
                  When you've learned how to cook and to fry.
                  Chop some wood, 'twill do you good,
                  And you'll eat in the sweet by and by.

JOE HILL

In 1926 Carl Sandburg wrote, "....Joe Hill is the only outstanding producer of lyrics widely sung in the militant cohorts of the labor movement of America. Jails and jungles from Lawrence, Mass. Woolen Mills to the Wheatland, California hop fields, have all heard the rhymes and melodies started by Joe Hill."

Notable songs in this category are his version of "Casey Jones", "The Preacher And The Slave" (tune—"Sweet Bye And Bye"), "Hallelujah, I'm A Bum" (Joe's version), "The Rebel Girl", and "Workers Of The World, Awaken". "The Rebel Girl" was dedicated to Elizabeth Gurley Flynn.

Joe Hill was executed on November 19th, 1915, on a trumped up murder charge, but his songs are still alive. They are models of adaptation of the typical American humor and "pop" style of his period, to the songs of and for the labor movement. Elizabeth Gurley Flynn, a personal friend of Joe's and a leader in his defense, sums it up this way:

"Joe Hill (Joseph Hillstrom), of Swedish birth, was a Western migratory worker. The I.W.W.'s of that day were young, robust, and militant. Joe was ardent and romantic, and although he was a good mechanic, preferred to stay with the 'Wobblies.' His greatest joy was to 'rattle the box' (play the piano) at I.W.W. affairs and compose his now famous songs." Joe Hill, Richard Frazier, Paul Brennan, T-Bone Slim (his song "The Popular Wobbly" is included in this bulletin), Ralph Chaplin, and many others are all part of this tradition inherited by People's Songs, Inc.

Joe Hill's version of "Hallelujah, I'm A Bum", an old Wobbly song, is a good example of the type of lyric writing which has made his songs so well loved. Our bulletin carried a modern parody on this tune in the 8th issue, song number 75, ("Hallelujah, I'm A-Travellin'). Here is the Joe Hill lyric:

"Oh, why don't you work
            like other men do?"
How can I work when there's
            no work to do?
Hallelujah, I'm a bum....
            (as in original)

A lady came out when I
            knocked on the door,
"You'll get nothing here
            'Cause I've seen you before"
"Oh, why don't you pray
            for your daily bread?"
If that's all I did,
            I'd be mighty soon dead,
"Oh, why don't you save
            all the money you earn?"
If I didn't eat, I'd have
            money to burn.

Aubrey Haan, a scholar at the University of Utah in Salt Lake City, is writing a novel based on the life and trial of Joe Hill. In this novel he will definitely prove the frame-up character of the trial, and Joe Hill's innocence. Included will undoubtedly be all the words to his songs. As soon as the book is released, we will announce it in our bulletin.

Waldemar Hille

WE continue our series of recorded interviews of workers and their songs. Some of our greatest American folk songs—songs with guts and feelings—recount experiences of those who have settled here. There's "Pat Works On The Railway" for one. But many of them never get beyond "the ghetto." This month Eduardo Reyes of New York City describes (1) how he wrote "Problema Social," (2) the Birth of La Conga and (3) the famous "Lamento Borincano." Transcribed by Francis Dellorco.

Problema Social —By Eduardo Reyes   1.

I decided to write a lyric that would make people happy and let them dance more because of the music and rhythm—but which would also bring home a message about the very great truths in the people's lives.

Yo, que peleaba en la guerra
Americano al fin, como nací.
Aunque sirvo pa' pelear
Yo no puedo votar
Pa' el presidente de la patria
Y al venir a trabajar
    (Repeat Chorus)

TRANSLATION

From a little island in the Carribean,
I came to the good old U.S. A.
But what a shock I got...
I find that I am not...
Welcome in my good old country,
Excepting to get shot!

CHORUS:
Look at me now, I'm a problem!
Boy, oh boy... isn't that a hot one?
Now... I'm called 'minority',
A real problem in sociology.
All I want is to earn enough pay
So I can feed my little family.
I don't want charity...I don't shirk,
All I want is just a chance to work.

Remember when I fought in the Army?
I'm an American, born and bred.
The gun I had to tote...
Did not get me a vote...
For president of my country;
And when I ask for work...
    (Repeat Chorus)

2. BIRTH OF LA CONGA

There was slavery in Cuba—about 1870 I'd say. Once a year the slaves were allowed to hold a comparsa. On that one day the slaves were free to do anything they wanted and they usually got drunk.

The comparsa was a group of dancers, 16 men and 16 women. They'd have a business, a pole with candles and paper streamers on it. The guy at the head would carry that, twirling it in the air, with the others dancing behind him. They originated their own step. This was how the Conga began.

They danced with machetes in their hands. It was the day they were free to show their strength. Stripped to the waist, wearing sashes, and their big field hats, the men would dance and sweat. The women wore fancy costumes.

Sometimes the whole comparsa would dress in exaggerated costumes mimicking what the masters wore. If the master wore a high hat, theirs would be twice as high and wide. If he wore a white tailcoat with satin lapels, theirs would be down to the ground and all satin. If he wore a bow tie, they'd wear bigger ones.

In 1898 the slaves got what is called freedom. La Conga carries on.

3. LAMENTO BORINCANO

"Lamento Borincano" by Rafael Hernandez is dear to every Porto Rican. Borinquen is the true name of the island of Porto Rico.

It is early in the morning
The sun is coming over the mountains;
Purples, yellows, lavenders are forming
    in the sky
Reflected off the clouds over the sea.
    A farmer is taking produce to market
    And as he goes he walks and thinks
      of this song to the beat
    Of the hooves of his little mare
He is happy, and he sings in his heart
About the wonderful feeling he is
    going to have
When he gets to market and sells his wares
And takes the money and buys a dress
To take home to his wife, La Viajita.
    He reaches town, now, and finds
      the place deserted;
    Everybody seems to be dead;
    There is nobody in the market
      to buy his produce

He is going back home.
The music is the same, but
Now he doesn't sing, he cries;
He thinks and walks
And he says in his heart:
    'This island, this beautiful island
    Of which the poet wrote and called
      the pearl of the sea
    Has been turned into a horrible thing!
    What will happen to my children,
      my wife?'
'Borinquen, now that you are dying
    from your suffering
Let me sing a song of sadness
    to you also.'

Go tell

Aunt Nancy
Aunt Rhodie
Aunt Abbie
The People

American folk song
New labor song version

There are lots of versions to this song: Go Tell Aunt Nancy, Aunt Abbie, Aunt Rhodie, and "especially the people." Here is the old folk song with a new version about the Taft-Hartley Bill. The adaptation was made at a labor song jam-session at the University of Wisconsin School for Workers, summer of 1947. Tom Glazer brought it to us and sang it at Town Hall some time ago, but it still seems to be about the best song on this subject.

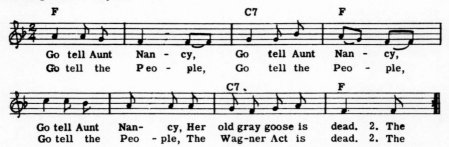

Go tell Aunt Nan - cy, Go tell Aunt Nan - cy,
Go tell the Peo - ple, Go tell the Peo - ple,

Go tell Aunt Nan - cy, Her old gray goose is dead. 2. The
Go tell the Peo - ple, The Wag-ner Act is dead. 2. The

(Folk song version)
The one she's been savin' . . .
To make a feather bed.

She died last Friday . . .
With an achin' in her head.

Old gander's weepin' . . .
Because his wife is dead.

The goslins are mournin' . . .
Because their mother's dead.

Go tell Aunt Nancy . . .
The old gray goose is dead.

(Union version)
The one we've been saving . . .
To keep our children fed.

It died in Congress . . .
When Taft cast off its head.

The people are crying . . .
Because their freedom is dead.

We'll keep on fighting . . .
We shall not be misled.

We will remember . . .
What Taft and Hartley said.

We'll vote out this Congress . . .
Put Labor in instead.

SINGING PEOPLE

●Woody Guthrie writes: "Cisco and myself sung the 'Henry Wallace Man' song at two rallies in Syracuse over the weekend, and one up at Cornell. The crowd liked the song pretty well, seemed like. (Sold lots of record albums at these three places and a good pile of songbooks, never less than $27 worth at a meeting of sixty or eighty people, which was a good sale, considering the sizes of the crowds.) They're really alive as to what's going on around the world, and hungry for songbooks and records that have a labor message.

All for this dime,
Woody Guthrie "

...John Crosby, radio columnist for the N.Y. Herald Tribune, heard some pickets singing and said, "so far as I know, this is the first use of the singing commercial in a labor dispute". Where did you go to school, John? Ever heard of the "Union Maid"?....The N.Y. Herald Tribune reported recently that a rare copy of the Bay Psalm book of 1640 was sold to a collector for $151,000. Hang on to your bulletins....

Alan Lomax's class in History of American Folk Music at N.Y.U. made newspaper columns last month when the classroom was discovered to be Cafe Society downtown which is not otherwise used on Monday nights by the club.

The Dean's office hastened to point out that the course, which is non-matriculated, was located at the night club in order that the noise of both the folk songs, and the jazz sessions that follow, would not interfere with other classes being held at the same time.

There is neither bar nor kitchen service on Monday nights, and students must get their inspiration from the music alone!

In the discussion on booking fees at the convention's performer's forum, someone retold the story of Woody Guthrie's answer to a woman who had asked him to do a benefit performance — 'since this was for a good cause.' 'Lady,' replied Woody, 'We don't sing for BAD causes.'

WOODY GUTHRIE THE SECOND

CONGRATULATIONS to Woody and Marjorie Guthrie. The new addition is a boy, named Arlo. Rumors are that Arlo is already refusing to be Pushed Around (see 'Songs to Grow On', page 3).

Most unusual booking of the year: Piute Pete calling square dances at a nudist camp. P. S.—It was a cold evening, and everybody was fully dressed.

In a midwest court this spring a Farm Equipment Union organizer was up on charges of using a sound truck at a strike-bound plant. The lawyer explained that the truck was being used to broadcast union songs.

"Why songs?" asked the puzzled judge. "Are they stimulating?"

Very much so, he was assured—— whereupon he asked the lawyer if he would please sing some for the court.

"I'm afraid, your honor," replied the lawyer, "that if you heard me sing you'd give my client the maximum sentence."

Case dismissed.

A member in West Pennsylvania reports coming across an old Dutch Reformed Church hymnbook with the following song in it: "When will you save the people, Lord; not the kings and rulers, but the people?"

THIS IS A STORY TOLD TO Richard Dyer Bennet by Augustine — who makes guitar strings for Dyer-Bennet and Segovia. The story came to us from Elynor Walden, who got it from Jeppy Madison, to whom Dyer-Bennet told it (this is known as 'the folk process').

Segovia was rehearsing for a concert when his bass E string—of which there was only one other in the world—broke. He called up Augustine to get the other string to him at once.

Augustine proceeded to look for the string which he had completed some time before. After an unsuccessful and frantic search, he suddenly recalled why he was not going to find it.

One day, he had noticed a little man dressed in faded dungarees standing with his wife in Tatay's guitar shop gazing longingly at the guitars which were apparently priced beyond his means.

Augustine was so moved that he called the man's wife aside and pressed Segovia's string into her hands, saying, 'When your husband feels discouraged because he cannot have a Tatay guitar, give him this.'

As the man and his wife left, Augustine watched, puzzling over an inscription painted across the face of the guitar:

THIS MACHINE KILLS FASCISTS

* * *

Confirmation from Woody:

The pair of (only) E strings (wound bass) are now owned by Segovia and me.

(Or was)   —W.G.

If you haven't yet heard. Kay Starr's "Sharecropper Blues" (Capitol) next time you're near a music store drop in and play it; it's right on the beam.

We'd be interested in knowing what People's Songs members think of the new Jo Stafford album of folk songs (Capitol) which is incidentally selling very well. She got the idea for recording the album following one of her radio programs on which she sang "Black Is the Color of My True Love's Hair". The accompaniment is very smooth, and some would consider it too slick. What's your opinion?

Among the recent Decca re-issues is the Carter family classic, "Coal Miner's Blues".

One of the first of the millionaire commercial hillbilly singers and composers, Vernon Dalhart, died last month at 65. "His Prisoners Song" (If I Had the Wings of an Angel) of '26 sold 25,000,000 copies.

What's the origin of the word "calypso"? The Duke of Iron, who should know, tells us that it was once "cariso" back in the 19th century days when everyone on Trinidad spoke French. During the thirties, when Yankee recording companies wanted a term for the distinctive local music, they chose the word we all know now from among the many dialect versions.

Michael Loring has become famous in Portland, Oregon, for singing "Roll On, Columbia". However, when he recently went to sing for the releif of the Vanport flood disaster victims, the chairman approached him with a glint in his eye and said, "Mr. Loring, there's one song we think you'd better not sing tonight . . ."

Senator Taft heard so many singing picketlines on his trip around the country that he eventually got to know some of our best People's Songs by heart, and when the correspondents on the train started singing "Union Maid" he hesitated a moment and then joined in on the chorus. Can't say it did much good, though.

A People's Songs member from Washington State says that "Acres Of Clams" (printed in Vol. 1, No. 9) used to be their State song, until some of the newer settlers thought it too undignified.

-- William Steig

Bob Claiborne relates that recently he went to a party where he met a political gentleman from Arkansas. Bob sang the song "State of Arkansaw". The politician who was by that time leering to veeward, promptly telephoned by long distance to the Governor-elect of Arkansaw, in Little Rock and held the phone while Bob sang the song. Said the Gov.-elect: "That's a fine song!" And added, pathetically, "I wish I was up there with you fellers, I'd be havin' a heap more fun than I'm havin' now." Both Arkansans overlooked the fact that the song is basically anti-Arkansas. Witness the line:

If you ever see me back again
I'll extend to you my paw,
But it'll be through a telesco-o-o-o-ope
From hell to Arkansaw!

New York.- Three people's songsters did a show at a union hall. In the course of an impromptu debate over the "correct" version of an old song with many variants, "The Farmers Curst Wife", with the three singers claiming that the Arkansas, Texas, and North Carolina versions were each the only true version, one of the girl singers called out, "There are no virg-- versions, that is from Texas!"

One of the most interesting new commercial hillbilly songs is "Hitler Lives" by Red River Dave, Texas radio singer. Since last fall, when he made it up, he has had more requests for it than any other song he is currently singing. Rosalie Allen waxed it for Victor last month, and more recordings will probably follow. Gist of idea: if you treat your fellow man unfairly, Hitler's still alive. If you forget the men who fought, and why: Hitler lives.

Some of the younger New York People's Songsters are now heard weekly on station WNYC on Oscar Brand's regular Sunday night folk music program. The singers and instrumentalists, from the American Folksay Group, include Fred Hellerman, Joe Jaffe, Ernie Lieberman, Tom Paley and Paul Turok.

PEOPLE'S PANCAKES? The newly-established People's Artists Bureau of Philadelphia books not only singers, instrumentalists, and square dancers -- but also a cook! The chef, a man with a reputation for making the most delicious progressive pancakes in the Quaker City, has decided to book exclusively through People's Songs.

ORCHIDS FROM THE SCRIBES

The New York Newspaper Guild holds an annual ball, one of the swankiest of the season. This year's, at the Waldorf Astoria, had such notables as the two Henry's Wallace and Morgan, Mayor O'Dwyer, and a regular milky way's worth of stars. 'Lo and behold, who should receive honorable mention (among others) but People's Songs Inc. (See Cut).

THE NEWSPAPER GUILD OF NEW YORK

Honors. People's Songs as

A Page One Must
for its notable songfests
in a democratic key

PAGE ONE BALL
Waldorf-Astoria
January 6, 1947

The favorite People's Song among the New Mexico Indians with whom Jenny Wells has been working in San Cristobal is 'Toom Balalaika.'

Al Moss, NY People's Songster, has opened the Sheridan Clam Bar, a new sea-food restaurant in Greenwich Village.

Ralph's, large Los Angeles Market, refused to hire Negro help. People's Songs members helped liven up the picketline that was thrown around it. Shirley Gray even went down to help keep up the morale of the graveyard shift, at 3 A.M. one night.

EDITORIAL

How long will it be before union songs and people's songs get put on juke boxes? It has already been done in many places: In Benton Harbor, Michigan, union members put "Talking Union" on the machines. And N.M.U. members used to take "The Ballad Of Harry Bridges" and get it on the music machines of waterfront bars all over the world, even as far afield as Australia. There ought to be more of this.

In Zurich, Switzerland, a friend reports hearing beer-hall entertainers who improvised songs giving the low-down on the news of the day, including personal satire a la Winchell and information on who slept with whom, etc. Calypso singers, who carry the news and editorials in their songs throughout the West Indies, have achieved quite a standard in that part of the world. Atilla The Hun has been elected to the Trinidad City Council, and was one of the brightest and most studious boys in school, according to teachers who remember him.

* * *

Serbian ballad singers used to interject military information into their long epic songs, a musicologist tells us. This was when they were fighting to rid their country of the Turks, and information had to be relayed to guerillas in the hills.... There is a great tradition of satirical poetry both in Africa and Arabia; a poet could neatly murder a local potentate if he wanted to. So in Arabia when a king put a poet on his payroll, they used to call it "cutting off the tongue of the poet".

Bart Van Der Schelling, well known especially on the West Coast for his singing of anti-fascist songs, says that he found a Welsh miners song which is a direct ancestor of "Peat Bog Soldiers". Only a few of the words were changed to make the famous concentration camp song.

WOODY GUTHRIE - A Book Review

American Folksong. A collection of poems and other writings by Woody Guthrie. Published by Disc Company of America, 117 West 46th St., New York, N.Y. $1.00. (Order through People's Songs.)

When Woody was in high school he learned how to typewrite. He sat in the school room looking out across the Oklahoma prairie and wishing he was out there chasing around and learning and finding out, and he started to put down just what he was thinking. He's been doing it ever since, and I guess he's written his way through several feet of typewriter paper by now. Some of you may have read his book "Bound For Glory" (E.P. Dutton, 1943). Here is a collection of some 35 songs and stories about himself and his friends, which you will want to read from cover to cover. There is no music printed, but if you have heard his records, you can pick up the tune; besides, this is printed like high class poetry, which you're supposed to read.

We were in a plane once, bound for Pittsburgh to sing for a couple thousand striking Westinghouse workers. While the rest of us were snoozing, biting our nails, worrying about debts, dreaming up big wishes, there was Woody, looking out the window and making up verse after verse about the plane, the stewardess, the ground below, the union folks we were bound for, and the beautiful country this could be.

Like thousands of other balladmakers, Woody never pretended to make up everything whole cloth; he'd take a little of the best of the old, and add something new. He once said, "Everything I know I learned off the kids." And it was in the speech of ordinary working people that he found his voice.

Peter Seeger

TWO EARLY LABOR SONGS

by Philip S. Foner, author of
"History of the Labor Movement in
the United States"

Below are two songs of the American labor movement: one written in 1860 and the other in 1868. The first, "The Shoemaker's Song," was written during the great Shoemaker's strike in New England which started in Lynn and Natick, Massachusetts, on February 22 1860 and rapidly spread throughout the state, into New Hampshire, Maine and Connecticut. By the end of the month, shoeworkers' unions were organized in at least twenty-five New England towns and close to 20,000 shoeworkers were on strike. It was the biggest strike in American history prior to the Civil War and gained nation-wide attention. Newspapers all over the country carried glaring headlines—'The Revolution in the North, 'The Rebellion among the Workmen of New England', 'The Shoemakers' Strike—Progress of the Social Revolution', 'Beginning of the Conflict between Capital and Labor.' It was in reference to the great shoe strike then in progress that Abraham Lincoln said at New Haven, March 6, 1860:

"I am glad to see that a system of labor prevails in New England under which laborers can strike when they want to, where they are not obliged to labor whether you pay them or not. I like the system which lets a man quit when he wants to, and wish it might prevail everywhere. One of the reasons why I am opposed to slavery is just here..."

The shoeworker's strike lasted for an entire month and resulted in an increase in wages for the workers.

The second song printed below, 'Eight Hours', was the most popular labor song in America during the late '60's, '70's and '80's. Although some unions raised the demand before and during the Civil War, the eight-hour movement began in earnest when the war was over. Under the leadership of Ira Steward of the Machinists and Blacksmiths Union, known as the father of the movement, and William H. Sylvis, president of the National Molders' Union, the struggle for the eight-hour day made rapid headway. Congress passed a law on June 25, 1868 providing an 8-hour day for laborers, mechanics and all other workmen in federal employ. By the end of the year, six states and several cities passed eight-hour laws. Mr Blanchard's song with original music by Rev. Jesse H. Jones was written during the campaign for these laws. The song remained popular even after the laws, due to various loopholes in the legislation, proved to be practically worthless. During the 1880's, when the labor movement shifted to strike action to secure the eight hour day, the song was revived. It became the official song of the eight-hour movement which culminated in the great demonstration on May 1, 1886—the first May Day in the history of the world labor movement.

THE SHOEMAKER'S SONG

Written for strikers - 1860
by Allen Peabody, Wenham, Mass.
To the tune of "Yankee Doodle"

Ye jours and snobs thru-out the land,
'Tis time to be astir;
The Natick boys are all on hand,
And we must not demur.

CHORUS:
Up and let us have a strike
Fair prices we'll demand.
Firmly let us all unite,
Unite thru-out the land.

This winter past, we've kept alive,
By toiling late at night,
With no encouragement to thrive
Such unpaid toil ain't right. (CHO.)

Starvation looks us in the face,
We cannot work so low;
Such prices are a sore disgrace;
Our children ragged go. (CHO.)

Our children must attend the schools,
And we must pay our bills,
We must have means to buy our tools,
Gaunt stomachs must be filled. (CHO.)

We must have decent clothes to wear,
A place to get our rest.
Must not be burdened so with care,
And must go better dressed. (CHO.)

Shall we run constantly in debt,
And toil the while like slaves?
Old age may overtake us yet-
May yet fill pauper's graves. (CHO.)

Shame on the men, the stupid curs,
Who might speak if they could,
Who will not join the Union boys,
But whine, '"Twill do no good."(CHO.)

The carpenters get up a strike
The masons do the same,
And we'll take hold with all our might,
And elevate our name. (CHO.)

'Twas union gained the glorious boon,
Our nation now enjoys;
Then let's awake and soon back up-
The glorious Natick boys. (CHO.)

Eight Hours

Words by I. G. Blanchard
Music by Rev. Jesse H. Jones
Anno - 1868

We mean to make things o-ver, We are tired of toil for naught, With but bare e-nough to live up-on And ne'r an hour for thought; We want to feel the sun-shine, And we want to smell the flowers, We are sure that God has willed it, And we mean to have eight hours. We're sum-mon-ing our for-ces from the ship-yard, shop, and mill.

CHORUS

Eight hours for work, Eight hours for rest,

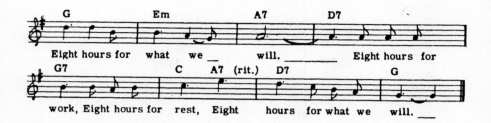

Eight hours for what we __ will. _____ Eight hours for

work, Eight hours for rest, Eight hours for what we will. __

The beasts that graze the hillside, and the birds that wander free,
In the life that God has meted, have a better lot than we.
Oh hands and hearts are weary, and homes are heavy with dole;
If our life's to be filled with drudgery, what need of a human soul.
  Shout, shout the lusty rally, from shipyard, shop, and mill.
  (CHORUS)

Ye deem they're feeble voices that are raised in labor's cause?
But bethink ye of the torrent, and the wild tornado's laws.
We say not toil's uprising in terror's shape will come,
Yet the world were wise to listen to the monetary hum.
  Soon, soon the deep toned rally shall all the nations thrill.
  (CHORUS)

From factories and workshops in long and weary lines,
From all the sweltering forges, and from out the sunless mines,
Wherever toil is wasting the force of life to live
There the bent and battered armies come to claim what God doth give,
  And the blazon on the banner doth with hope the nation fill:
  (CHORUS)

Hurrah, hurrah for labor, for it shall arise in might;
It has filled the world with plenty, it shall fill the world with light.
Hurrah, hurrah for labor, it is mustering all it's powers
And shall march along to victory with the banner of Eight Hours.
  Shout, shout the echoing rally till all the welkin thrill:
  (CHORUS)

VENIT.

UAW-CIO

Words and Music by Butch Hawes
Copyright 1942, by the Almanac Singers

Nearly every union wishes they had a song they could call all their own; few
have a better one than this. In 1942 the Almanac Singers were living in Detroit
and singing for locals of the UAW. It was in the days when conversion to war pro-
duction was urgent. Some people have suggested changing the words in view of
changed times, but the consensus seems to be: let it stand, a good song true to
its time

I was standing down on Gra-tiot St. one day. When I
thought I ov-er heard a sol-dier say: "Ev- ry tank & plane in camp carries that
U. A. W. stamp & I'm U. A. W. too I'm proud to say.
Chorus (double-u)
It's that U. A. W. C. I. O. makes that ar-my roll & go
turn-in' out the jeeps & tanks, the air-planes ev'ry day, It's that
U. A. W. C. I. O.- makes that ar-my roll and go,
Puts wheels on the U. S. A.

I was there when the union came to
  Town.
I was there when old Henry Ford went
  down.
I was standing at Gate Four
When I heard the people roar,
"Ain't nobody keeps us union workers
  down." (Chorus)

I was there on that cold December day
When we heard about Pearl Harbor,
  far away.
I was down at Cadillac Square

When the union rallied there
To put those plans for pleasure cars
  away. (Chorus)

There'll be a union label in Berlin
When the union boys in uniform march
  in.
And rolling in the ranks
There'll be UAW tanks,
Roll Hitler out and roll the union in.
  (Chorus)

Capitalistic Boss

Words by Mike Stratton
Music by Saul Aarons
Cop.1948 Stratton-Aarons

During the late thirties the songwriting team of Mike Stratton and Sol Aarons turned out several hits which will no doubt last for many years to come. "Picket Line Priscilla" and "Horse with the Union Label" have already been printed in past issues of this bulletin. The song on this page is of course a performance number which when done well makes devastating satire.

I'm the much ma-ligned Cap-i-tal-is-tic Boss.
(D.S -fine) much ma-ligned Cap-i-tal-is-tic Boss,
Ev-ery night up-on my bed I toss,
Ev-ery night up-on my bed I toss,
"Cause the reds keep both-er-ing me, They just can't see
'Cause with all the mon-ey I've got, If you think I'm
letting me be, Ev-en in my dreams they're with me, And my
hap-py, I'm not, For, I love my work-ers a lot; Yet I
dreams as such Are much too much for me to
treat them so, Oh, I don't know, I'm real-ly
bear, The care is driv-in' me nuts, It's
good at heart But some-thing is tear-ing me
most un-fair. wide a-part! (1.) I am on-ly
hu-man e-ven as you and you, Da-dee-ah,
da-dee-ah And I can-not help it
No more than you or you, The things I do I can't ex-

C   A♭7   G7   C   G7

plain,   Some-thing is wrong with my   brain —

C   G7

Money fills my helpless head with   fierce intoxication

Cm   G7

Feeble in it's fiendish grip, Oh,   fatal fascination, I

Cm   C dim

can't resist the awful urge I   feel within me rising, And

C# dim   G7

then transformed when I emerge. I'm   past all recognizing, My

Cm   G7   Cm   G7

stomach is a   bloated sight I   wear a silk hat day and night. I

Cm

ride around in Cadillacs, I   trample on the workers backs. I

G7

chisel on my income tax, My God! The things I   do.

C   A♭7   G7

I can't ex - plain.   Some-thing is wrong with my

1.2.3. C   4 C

brain.   brain.   I'm the   D. S. al fine

(2.) Take my wife for instance, really she's not so bad.
She was but a dairy maid, and I a lad,
And so we wed, I can't explain;
Something is wrong with my brain.
Her father was the president of Milk Incorporated
He taught his own contented cows to give evaporated,
Though captain of his industry he doted on his daughter,
And made her heir to grade "B" milk
Dissolved in grade "A" water.
I was a poor but honest lad
Her bovine beauty drove me mad
Her tender lips , her sable coat,
The gem she wore around her throat.
That gem she wore around her throat, MY GOD!
And so we wed, I can't explain;
Something is wrong with my brain.

72

(3) When it comes to labor, that's where I'm really fair;
After all t'was labor made me a millionaire,
And yet we fight, I can't explain;
Something is wrong with my brain.
I cut their wages every day, it gives me such a pleasure,
I disregard the men that say they haven't any leisure;
I always work them overtime without an extra penny,
And if they ask for two weeks off, I just don't give them any.
And when they strike, I clamp down hard,
Protected by the National Guard.
I raise a patriotic stink, I call in every first class fink,
Descendant from the missing link, MY GOD!
And yet we fight, I can't explain;
Something is wrong with my brain!

(4) Take my son for instance, he is my pride and joy,
Quite a likely youngster, really a clever boy.
The things he does, I can't explain;
Something is wrong with his brain.
I give him his allowance but it's not enough for buttons,
He has to have a yacht of two to keep up with the Huttons.
You don't know what a lot it costs to keep a polo pony,
And though he has no income tax,
There's always alimony.
His social life's a giddy whirl
From debutante to chorus girl,
He never sleeps he never sits,
By winter he's so shot to bits,
He has to go to Biarritz, MY GOD!
The things he does, I can't explain;
Something is wrong with his brain.

If there had been space, we would
have printed a whole page-full of the
cartoons of Art Young, the man who
made the top-hatted, pot-bellied cap-
italist so well known in the early Socia-
list newspapers thirty and forty years
ago.

Wasn't That A Time

Words and music by
Lee Hays and
Walter Lowenfels

"Wasn't That a Time", really ought to be called "Isn't This a Time", for it tries to say that these are tough wonderful times to live and work and fight in. During the recent months of campaigning, people's songsters have been singing the rythmic tunes of the new party, like "Passing Through". Of them all, only a few are reflective songs which try to say more than can be said in a jingle. The writers of this song have attempted to say things for November and the months that lie ahead. It is being sung by the American People's Chorus in New York and will undoubtedly be used by other choruses and singers across the land. Don't let its apparent irregularities baffle you. It actually is a four line verse and a four line chorus and could be typed to look very much like "Solidarity Forever". The music, however, uses changes of tempo to heighten the developing ideas of the verses. We hope that this song will start a trend among songwriters toward somewhat more serious musical treatments of issues of the day in these "times that try men's souls".

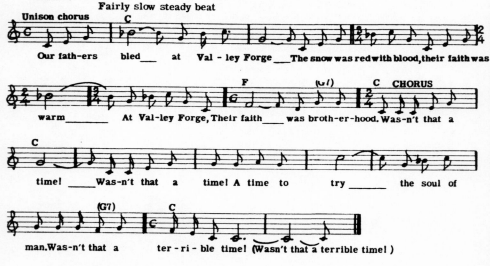

Our fath-ers bled___ at Val - ley Forge ___ The snow was red with blood, their faith was warm____ At Val-ley Forge, Their faith___ was broth-er-hood. Was-n't that a time! ____ Was-n't that a time! A time to try ____ the soul of man. Was-n't that a ter-ri-ble time! (Wasn't that a terrible time!)

Brave men who fought...
at Gettysburg...
now lie in soldiers' graves,
But there they stemmed...
the rebel tide
and there...the faith was saved.
  Wasn't that a time!
  Wasn't that a time!
  A time to try the soul of man!
  Wasn't that a terrible time!

The fascists came...
with chains and war...
to prison us in hate.
And many a good...
man fought and died
to save...the stricken faith.
  Wasn't that a time!
  Wasn't that a time!
  A time to try...the soul of man!
  Wasn't that a terrible time!

And now again...
the madmen come...
and shall our victory fail?
There is no vic...tory
in a land
where free...men go to jail.
Isn't this a time!
Isn't this a time!
A time to try...the soul of man!
Isn't this a terrible time!

Our faith cries out....
THEY SHALL NOT PASS! ...
We cry NO PASARAN!
We pledge our lives,...
our honor, all
to free...this prisoned land.
Isn't this a time!
Isn't this a time!
A time to FREE...
the soul of man!
Isn't this a wonderful time!
Isn't this a wonderful time!

The Four Maries

Scottish, 16th Century
Words as sung by
Betty Sanders, NYC

One of the most beautiful of the old Scottish ballads, this song springs from a known historical incident, when one of the handmaidens of Mary, Queen of Scots, was discovered to be consorting with her boss' lover, and was paid quite promptly for her indiscretion.

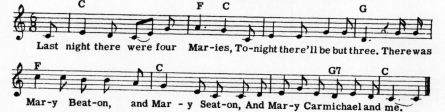

Last night there were four Mar-ies, To-night there'll be but three. There was
Mar-y Beat-on, and Mar-y Seat-on, And Mar-y Carmichael and me.

Oh often have I dressed my queen
And put on her braw silk gown,
But all the thanks I've got tonight,
Is to be hanged in Edinburgh town.

Full often have I dressed my queen,
Put gold upon her hair,
But I have got for my reward
The gallows to be my share.

They'll tie a kerchief around my eyes
That I may not see to dee,
And they'll never tell my father or mother,
But that I'm across the sea.　(Repeat first verse)

SWINGIN' ON A SCAB

(From the Los Angeles picket lines)

A scab is an animal that walks on his
  knees
He sniffs every time the bosses sneeze
His back is brawny but his brain is
  weak
He's just plain stupid with a yellow
  streak
But if you don't care whose back it is
  you stab
Go right ahead and be a scab

(Cho):
  Are you gonna stick on the line
  Till we force the bosses to sign
  This is your fight brother, and mine
  —Or would you rather be a fink?

A fink is an animal that smells like a
  skunk
He's two brackets lower than a punk
He makes his living out of breaking
  strikes
Cause busting unions is a job he likes
But if you get so you kinda like the
  stink
Go right ahead and be a fink!

(Cho) —Or would you rather be a stool

A stool is an animal with long hairy
  ears
He runs back with everything he hears
He's no bargain though he can be
  bought
And though he's slippery he still gets
  caught
But if your brain's like the rear end of
  a mule
Go right ahead and be a stool!

(Cho) —Or would you rather be a goon

A goon is an animal that's terribly shy
He can't stand to look you in the eye
He rides to work on the cops' coat-
  tails
And wears brass knuckles to protect
  his nails
But if your head is like the hole in a
  spitoon
Go right ahead and be a goon!

(Final Chorus):

You don't have to lead with your chin
You can pick your side and pitch in
Cause the union's going to win. . .
Until the day the bosses sign—
We're gonna stick right on the line!

Peace on Earth

Music by Hans Eisler
New words by Lee Hays
Four Part Round

The Same Merry-Go-Round

Words and music by Ray Glaser and Bill Wolff
Copyright 1948 by Ray Glaser and Bill Wolff

Try this cute little merry-go-round tune with steam calliope effects. It was written by the same team that produced "Put it on the Ground." Earl Robinson has been singing it with great effectiveness recently. For further details see cover.

The don-key is tired and thin, _____ The el-e-phant thinks he'll move in, _____ They yell and they fuss, But they ain't fool-in' us 'cause they're broth-ers right un-der the skin. _____

CHORUS

It's the same, same, mer-ry-go-round, Which one will you ride this year? _____ The don-key and el-e-phant bob up and down on the same mer-ry-go-round. _____

The Elephant comes from the North,
The Donkey may come from the South;
If you'll look you'll find -
The Donkey's behind -
But they got the same bit in their mouth!
(CHORUS)

If you want to end up safe and sound,
Get offa the Merry-go-round;
To be a real smarty
Just join the Third Party
And get your two feet on the ground!
(CHORUS ...'Cause it's the same . . .)

77

CORRESPONDENCE

Dear Editor:

I liked Lee Hays' piece in the Bulletin about folk music. My rule for music is that it has to be alive. Some things seem more alive than others, maybe in some special time and maybe forever. I admit the truth of the saying, "I don't know much about music but I like what I know." I used to go to the Methodist Church in Evanston to hear Bach played but had I had Woody and Josh at home (on records, I mean) I would have stayed away from Bach, because they are alive and I can understand more from them than I can from Bach, fine as he is.

As for your opera -- you have to be a pretty subtle character to make folk music out of that and you KNOW it. They are damn near all of them, that I know anything about, propaganda for Fascism. They are played for rich folks, they show man as a wretch and a scoundrel unless he is trained in the rules of existing society. Some people love the music. And the words they sing poison them. It's part of the system AND IT MAKES ME SICK.

B.R., Boise, Idaho

Dear All & Everybody:

I cant fly to the windy town today to sing the Abraham Lincoln show with Earl Robinson for the Civil Rights Committee, on account of they mailed my plane ticket to me on Monday so's it would get in my hand today by 8 a.m. this morning, but we didn't have no mail delivery today. It's Abe's birthday, a legal holiday all acrost the country. Because it's Abe's birthday I can't get my ticket to fly to Chicago to sing for him.

I spent several hours looking through the new People's Song Book. All of its 128 pages, from Lomax to Botkin, and on and on it gets better and better and ends up with a full page of highly needed guitar chords, which may have some big influence on making a Glen Taylor out of a Lee O'Daniel.

Marjorie likes the looks of the book and says it just fits on the business end of our piano. Our 7 month old son, Arlo Davy, says tell you that you sure did pick out a good flavor of glue and starch to use on that stiff back binding. Arlo and the book went to press at just about the same time. They're both able to sit up on their own powers alone. And the book and the baby are just about as loud, as plain, as clear, and as honest as each other.

I don't see any big changes which ought to be made in either one. Both sing. Both grow on you. Both will travel and go yonder. Both will make new friends. Both will make more friends for the Union.

Thanks again to every hand that had a finger in the job of getting this book out. Yes, thanks to Boni & Gaer, too— I'm not such a practiced hand at thanking publishers, but Boni & Gaer have both got thanks coming.

Thanks to several thousand hands and eyes around the globe that are just about to snatch this People's Song Book and hold it to their breast like a new found kid.

Woody Guthrie

Dear Barbara (% People's Songs)

I'm just a poor wayfaring stranger a looking for a home, a looking for a home.

When I was a bachelor, I gave my love a cherry. Black, black, black is the color of my true love's hair. I wonder as I wander to the House of the Rising Sun who's gonna shoe your pretty little feet marching down Freedom road.

Alas, my love, you do me wrong. Go way from my window and blow the candles out for this old world is in a sad condition and I ain't going to be treated this a-way.

Oh it's hard and it's hard ain't it hard to roll your leg over pretty little black eyed Suzie. You ought to see my Cindy for they call her the lass with the delicate air, but she left me with a bunch of water cresses in the garden where the praties grow.

Go tell Aunt Rhodie that I met her in Venezuela surrounded by acres of clams when John Henry was a little baby. I said, "Where do you come from, brother?" "Strange Fruit." Put it on the ground and fare thee well oh honey for I'm gonna lay me down and die do die.

Love,

Sweet William
Hotel Lafonda
Taos, New Mexico

Dear Editor,
    I'd like to register my protest to your taking up valuable space in the latest issue of the bulletin with the Guthrie rewrite of "Jessie James".
    Perhaps Guthrie can get away with singing it. His personality as a performer is such as to make it possible. But I can't imagine another singer who could do it...

    To some minds,singing the story of Jesus Christ in this manner, and being daringly outright and ostentatious about it is cute and clever. I'm no supporter of "purity and godliness"in dealing with the church and its fables, but I can see no point in offending people to whom sacrilage is of deep importance. And I mean working people- the people you are trying to reach. Cuteness and cleverness and flying in the face of convention do not by themselves make songs that will function as peoples songs should.
    We need more than the witty patter...Let's have more meat and potatoes and less cream fluff in our music. Sincerely,
                    Gladys Bashkin

Dear Editor,
    I read a letter from Gladys Bashkin in the bulletin calling the song "Jesus Christ" a waste of space. I sang it in my barracks one evening, and noticed that the gang was showing an interest in the song. Some of them came over and asked for a repeat (and my name isn't Woody Guthrie,Gladys).
    I personally believe that the song is more than "cute". I've always looked at it as a condemnation of the people who corrupt Christ's teachings Pvt. J.B. Wiener
                    Fort Bragg, N.C.

Dear People's Songs,

'Merry Xmas' —Ben Shahn

Dear People's Songs:

    There has been a crazy, incorrect story going around about a certain song, and it seems that this would be the best place to set things straight for the record!

    It concerns a "Philippine Guerilla Song" with the chorus, "To my gun, to my gun, to my thunderbolt." The first verse goes, "I'm a battling bastard from Bataan, no pop, no mom, no Uncle Sam". Fact is, this song was written in 1941 by the Almanac Singers when they read this couplet in a newspaper release about Bataan. Arthur Stern, one of the Almanac Singers at that time, heard me singing a Texas ox-drivers' song. He made up the rest of the verses and the chorus following that opening couplet.

    So now everywhere I go, people want to know if I've heard that wonderful "Philippine Guerilla Song".

                    Peter Seeger

To the Editor:
    A few months ago I kicked because I wasn't getting any letters from readers of my column, if any; so what happened? Right away you got a couple of letters. That's fine. The writers showed rare taste and judgment. I wish they had written me, so I could thank them personally and congratulate them upon their good sense.

    From now on, let all communications be addressed to me. I don't get enough mail, only letters from collection a-gencies, old sweethearts and docu-ments from the Library Guild, also re-jection slips and other such trash. I'd be happy to hear from everyone, es-pecially blondes, brunettes and auburn-haired. If there's anything in those let-ters which in my judgment deserves to be printed in the Bulletin, I'll be glad to pass them on to the editors. I will even go so far as to re-type the letters for greater legibility, and tidy up the grammar, and leave out sentences that don't make sense.

    I think in this way my fan mail is bound to increase, and you will see that fan letters will be written with more style and punch.

                    Lee Hays

Dear Sir,

Rcd. your letter of April 4 stating where a group of singers and musicians were throwing a benefit performance for the beloved Miners Widows and Orphans. Owing to all the work that had to be done and with the short of help, I am very sorry I could not answer sooner. As for a fund being set up, yes our City Mayor O.W. Wright has started a fund. Our Local, Union No. 52 also receives some donations direct which we handle through our Local Union Committee set up for that purpose without any salary whatsoever. Trusting this will explain everything. Enclosed you will find a song made up by Mr. and Mrs. Wm. E. Rowekamp. Sincerely yours,

Wm. E. Rowekamp
Rec. Secy. Local Union 52
Centralia, Illinois

THE SONG:-

Sing a song of a miner in a mine so deep,

Where a dreary labor is done and no one can see.

Work with picks and shovel busy all the day,

Never see the sunlight, not a single ray.

We should think with the miners you would all agree

Where the dreary work is done and none of us can see.

Editor's Note: As a result of the Miners' Benefit Hootenanny sponsored by People's Songs, $387.00 was collected and sent to Centralia.

Hello, Pete,

The news from People's Songs these days fills my heart with joy. Believe me, I am one that knows the value of labor songs. I have sung them and composed them and used them for years in teaching right from wrong. You are doing a great thing when you are teaching People's songs. It helps put so many workers in unions where every working man and woman belongs....

....I am proud of all our old Hootenanny crowd....so please keep on singing and keep your banjo ringing. Let's sing and ring out this old stuff and ring in something new that will bring peace and plenty all over the world.

Love as always
Aunt Molly Jackson
Sacramento, Cal.

Dear Sir:

Lee Hays never fooled me. All this Arkansas preacher, hobo, rough diamond stuff, I mean. A long way back I had him spotted for a poet and a critic, and an aesthete to boot. Now he proves it with his remarks about rhythm and rhyme. Amen, brother, Amen!

Not long ago someone wrote that poetry should be written to read or sing, not solve. I've done a lot of skirmishing on that front in the last few years. I've been able to help confirm the trend toward rhythm and rhyme in such top-flight people's poets as Aaron Kramer, Fred Blair, Martin Garnet and Gordon Murray. It isn't going to do a good cause a bit of harm to have Lee Hays enlisting in it.

For what Lee says makes sense. Maybe he'll let me suggest a clarifying notion or two. "Breathing, the flow of blood in our bodies, the way our limbs move...these are rhythm," says Lee. Right, but these are also meter. I chuckle at Lee's insinuation that one reason versifiers today shun meter is that it's hard work. But he seems to give up the field there too easily. No one knows better than Lee that when a song really gets under the skin, we show it by tapping our feet, or swaying our bodies, or clapping our hands. The poem not sung, not set to music, merely read or recited, which yet has metrical rhythm, if it does not set us tapping or clapping or swaying outwardly, nevertheless does so inwardly. Anyone can learn why just by putting his finger on his pulse: our blood flows not only rhythmically but metrically.

Now about rhyme. This was invented by the Irish "poets" of remote pagan times. They were really genealogists and annalists. They had to memorize thousands of lines of legend and tribal history. Same with other peoples -- the Jews invented repetition, the Greeks devised hexametric rhythm as memory-aids; the Irish hit on rhyme, the best memory-aid of all. If you want a song or a poem to be remembered, the surest way is to tip your lines with rhyme.

Yours lyrically,
Shaemas O'Sheel

Dear Ed.:

When I drink I feel, I feel
Visions of poetic zeal;
But drunker yet I get, and reel
On praise from Shaemas, The O'Sheel

—Lee Hays

"Dear Sir:

I have your reply saying that my song 'Love Me Today' is not your type of song. Frankly, I don't understand you. People sing my song wherever they hear it, and love it. ...If this isn't a Peoples Song I would like to know what you think is."

The Ballad For
Un-American Blues

Words and music by Lee Hays and Walter Lowenfels
Arranged by Waldemar Hille

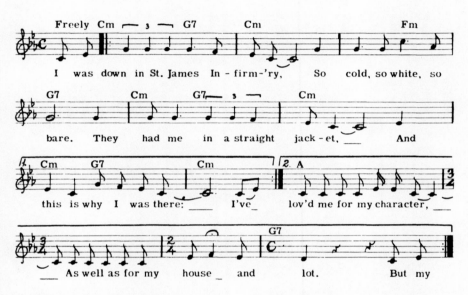

2. I've got me a million dollars,
   Also an ocean-going yacht;
   Once I had me a pretty woman,
   She swore she loved me for my character—
   as well as for my house and lot.

3. But my pretty woman has left me,
   My ever-loving woman has fled;
   She said, "I'll not stay married
   To a man that nobody calls a Red."

head. You may be sweet six-teen, and nev-er been kissed, But no-

bo-dy's gon-na love you If you ain't been called a Communist. You ain't no-

bo-dy at all, __ If no-bo-dy calls you a Red. __ Now if you

want to be suc -cess - ful __ In the mov-ies or the ra - di -

o. If you want to get a - head, You got to be a Red 'Cause

J. Par-nell Thom-as says so. Be-cause you just ain't no -

bo-dy at all __ If no-bo-dy calls you a Red.

If you go by what the pa - pers say There's one un-der ev-'ry

Interruption section, patterned after the "Ballad for Americans":

(Someone else)
bed. Now wait a minute. Who's a Red?

(Ballad singer)
Well . . . let me see. There's -
HENRY WALLACE, MRS. ROOSEVELT, SHIRLEY TEMPLE,
(add your own well-known local names)
Movie Writers, Radio Actors, Broadway Playwrights, Ballad Singers,
And that ain't all. . . There's also

Union Members, Organizers, Preachers, Teachers, Workers,
ALL OF THEM, They're a bunch of so-forths,
A lot of Reds!

(Someone else)
Is THAT what they say?

(Ballad singer)
They sure do. . . And that ain't all:

You ain't got no style, You ain't got no fame, If the

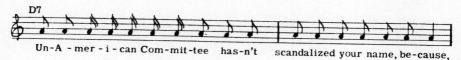

Un-A-mer-i-can Com-mit-tee has-n't scandalized your name, be-cause,

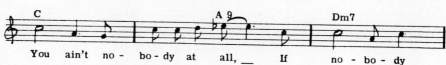

You ain't no-bo-dy at all, __ If no-bo-dy

calls you a Red!

Bob L.

THE DEATH OF HARRY SIMMS

By Jim Garland, as sung by
Aunt Molly Jackson

Come and lis-ten to my sto-ry come and lis-ten to my song; I will tell you of a he-ro that is now dead and gone. I will tell you of a young boy, whose age-was nine-teen; He was the brav-est un-ion man that I have ev-er seen.

Other verses:

Harry Simms was a pal of mine,
We labored side by side,
Expecting to be shot on sight,
Or taken for a ride,
 By the dirty coal operator gun thugs
 Who roam from town to town,
 A-shooting down the union men
 Where'er they may be found.

Harry Simms and I were parted
At five o'clock that day.
"Be careful, my dear comrade,"
To Harry I did say.
 "I must do my duty,"
 Was his reply to me.
 "If I get killed by gun thugs,
 Don't grieve after me."

Harry Simms was a-walkin' up the track
This bright sunshiny day;
He was a youth of courage,
His step was light and gay.
 We did not know the gun thugs
 Were hiding on the way,
 To kill our dear young comrade
 This bright sunshiny day.

Harry Simms was killed on Brush Creek
In nineteen thirty-two;
He organized the miners
Into the N.M.U.
 He gave his life in struggle,
 That was all that he could do,
 He died for the Union,
 Also for me and you.

THE STORY BEHIND THIS AMERICAN BALLAD

By Mary Elizabeth Barnacle
Professor of Folklore at NYU
and the Univ. of Tennessee

The strike in the soft coal camps in Bell County, Kentucky first started in 1931, mostly conducted by the rank and file of the UMWA--the officials giving no leadership; on the contrary, they helped to break the strike by betraying the miners. But the strike continued, taking on a new lease of life in January, 1932, under the guidance of the National Miners' Union.

Harry Simms, a young organizer from Springfield, Mass., nineteen years old, as tender-hearted as he was strong-minded, was at this time organizing in the South. Sometime in the winter of 1931 he came to Pineville and worked energetically and tirelessly among the young people of the NMU. He took an active part in the leadership of the strike. He made powerful speech after powerful speech. "Spell-binder", the miners called him. A good part of the time he stayed with Jim Garland, one of the main spark plugs of the strike, and with Tilmon Cadle, another native leader, and with other miners and their families. Not only did he put new heart into these hard-pressed men who had

"No food, no clothes for our children,
I'm sure this hain't no lie,
If we don't get more for our labor
We'll starve to death and die"

as Aunt Molly Jackson, (Jim Garland's sister) sang in her "Kentucky Miner's Wife's Hungry Ragged Blues", but he was out in front, filling every day with the maximum of perilous activity.

Word, in the course of the strike, came to the miners in Pineville that their friends outside of Kentucky were sending in five truck loads of food and clothing. These people wanted to test the democracy of Kentucky and to show that they could, as friends of the miners, come into this feudal area and distribute relief. They had called for a demonstration of the miners on the day of the arrival of the trucks and Harry Simms had been chosen to lead the miners out of Brush Creek to Pineville to get their share of the relief.

("Ragged and hungry, no slippers on our feet,
We're bumming around from place to place, to get a little bite to eat,"
as Aunt Molly's song wailed their wretchedness.)

Jim Garland, who loved Harry Simms as a brother, warned the latter against going up Brush Creek because gun-thugs were always running that road. Simms replied, "It's my job to lead the men to Pineville, and gun-thugs or no gun-thugs, I'll go. If they pop me off, don't waste time grieving after me, but keep right on going. We'll win." In the company of Green Lawson he set out. As they were walking up the road going to Brush Creek the jitney bus that runs along the railroad came along with two gun-thugs aboard. As soon as they spotted the two miners they jumped off the bus, their six-shooters smoking. Harry Simms fell. He was taken to the hospital at Barbourville. Four days later he died. On the very same day that he lay dead in Barbourville, the two gun-thugs were acquitted under the protection of 900 state troopers and 175 special police.

Despite all their troops and guns and state of martial law, the police at Barbourville were so terrified of a demonstration of the miners at this flagrant murder that they would not turn the body over to a separate person; only to a committee of three. They allowed no funeral to be held. "They was to be no talkin', no walkin', no marchin' behind that corpse there. The Committee was to put him on a train and get him out of there." The Committee--Tilmon Cadle, Gertrude Hessler, Jeff Franz--put the body of the radiant youth on the train to New York. He lay in state at a Coliseum in Manhattan. Jim Garland told the great crowds of mourners how Harry Simms had labored so unselfishly and so courageously in the bloody coalfields of Bell County, Kentucky. And then Jim wrote this song to his friend.

OUT OF YOUR POCKET

Words and Music by Bryant French
Copyright 1947 by Bryant French

Bryant writes: This summer I appeared along with Darel McConkey, author of the monopoly-exposing book "Out of your Pocket", at the district convention of the United Shoe Workers in Portsmouth, Ohio. As I was to come on just before McConkey, it was suggested that I introduce him. My job's singing songs, not making speeches, so I cooked up a little ditty—the present chorus of "Out of your Pocket"—and used it in place of introductory remarks. The darn thing kept going around in my head and before I knew it I was making up verses for it.

When I go buy some gro-ceries, I shell out lots of dough Oh, won't some-bo-dy tell me, please, Where does the mon-ey go? I nev-er get a taste of meat, And boy, I'm get-ting bored, 'Cause ev'-ry sing-le chop and steak's The one I can't af--ford.. Out of your pock-et, Out of your pock-et, Out of your pock-et, Oh, where does the mon-ey go? It goes in-to the pock-et, In-to the pock-et, In-to the pock-et Of the

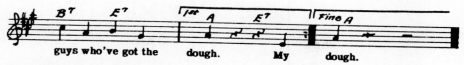

guys who've got the dough. My dough.

My rent is high, my cash is low,
And I'm caught in between.
My landlord drives the longest, fastest
Car you ever seen.
My walls are thin, my carpets too,
My ceilings are like sieves,
But you should see the lovely mansion
Where my landlord lives.
(CHORUS)

It doesn't seem quite fair to me
That I should dig so deep
To pay a guy who makes a half
A million in his sleep

I even can't afford a beer
For me it's pretty high,
Because I'm paying off my boss's
Fancy scotch and rye.
(CHORUS)

They tell me it's monopolies
Own everything I see,
So I'll be on the market soon
'Cause they own most of me.
And after they have processed me
And wrapped me up so nice,
They'll sell me right back to myself
At some gawd-awful price.

Raggedy

Tune From An Old Hymn
Words By John Handcox
Sharecropper Song, 1936

This is but one of many hymn-type labor songs that arose during the early 1930's when unionism swept through the south, affecting millions of sharecroppers and millworkers whose main musical experience had been spirituals and other hymn singing. "Roll The Union On", "We Shall Not Be Moved" and "Strange Things Happening In This Land" were all made up by students and teachers at Commonwealth College, in Mena, Arkansas. John Handcox, main originator of "Raggedy Are We" was a Negro sharecropper and a lay preacher on the side.

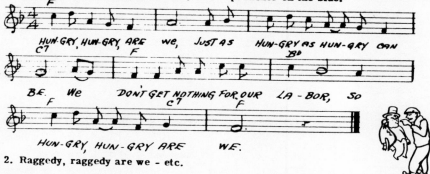

HUN-GRY, HUN-GRY, ARE we, JUST AS HUN-GRY AS HUN-GRY CAN
BE. We DON'T GET NOTHING FOR OUR LA-BOR, SO
HUN-GRY, HUN-GRY ARE WE.

2. Raggedy, raggedy are we - etc.

3. Homeless, homeless are we - etc.

4. Landless, landless are we - etc.

5. Angry, angry are we - etc.

6. Union members are we,
   Just as union as union can be,
   We're going to get something for our labor,
   So union members are we.

Go, Where I Send Thee

American Negro Folk
Arr. by Peter Seeger
Copyright 1946, People's Songs, Inc.

(this song is accumulative - adding new lines to previous
verse without a break - building up naturally)

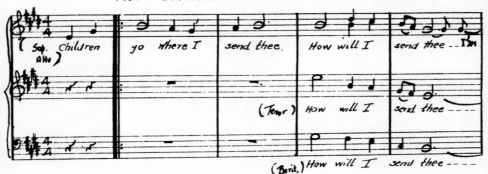

```
3's for Paul and / Silas
3's for the Hebrew / Children
4's for the 4 that / stood at the door
5's for the gospel preachers
6's for the 6 who / never got fixed
7's for the 7 that / never got to Heaven
8's for the 8 that / stood at the gate
9's for the 9 all / dressed so fine
10's for the 10 com / mandments....
```

*Always add previous verses at this point until all ten are accumulated. The last verse will run like this: "Children go where I send Thee, How will I send Thee, I'm a gonna send you 10 by 10, 10's for the 10 com/ mandments, 9's for the 9 etc., till "Little Bitty Baby, Born, Born, Born in Bethlehem."

Here is a Christmas song that is Choral in folk tradition. Sounds best in a small group, five good singers is plenty.

Jesus Christ

(Tune: Jesse James)
— Woody Guthrie

Copyright 1946, Woody Guthrie

Jesus Christ was a Man that traveled through the land,
Hard working Man and brave,
He said to the rich, give your goods to the poor,
So they laid Jesus Christ in His Grave.

Jesus was a Man, a Carpenter by Hand,
His followers true and brave;
One dirty coward called Judas Iscariot
Has laid Jesus Christ in His Grave.

He went to the Preacher, He went to the Sheriff,
Told them all the same;
Sell all of your jewelry and give it to the poor,
But they laid Jesus Christ in His Grave.

When Jesus came to town, the working folks around
Believed what He did say;
The bankers and the preachers they nailed him on a cross,
And they laid Jesus Christ in His Grave.

Poor working people, they follered him around,
Sung and shouted gay;
Cops and the soldiers they nailed Him in the air,
And they laid Jesus Christ in His Grave.

Well the people held their breath when they heard about His Death
Everybody wondered why;
It was the landlord and the soldiers that he hired,
That nailed Jesus Christ in the sky.

This song was written in New York City,
Of rich men, preachers and slaves;
If Jesus was to preach like he preached in Galilee,
They would lay Jesus Christ in His Grave.

The Dodger Song

As recorded by the Almanac Singers

Yes, the can-di-date's a dodg-er, yes a well known dodg-er, Yes the can-di-date's a dodg-er, yes and I'm a dodg-er too. He'll meet you and and treat you ask you for your vote, But look out boys, he's a-dodg-ing for a note! Yes, we're all dodg-ing, a - dodg-ing, dodg-ing, dodg-ing, Yes we're all dodg-ing out a-way through the world.

Oh the lawyer he's a dodger,
  Yes, a well-known dodger,
Oh the lawyer he's a dodger,
  Yes, and I'm a dodger, too.
He'll plead your case and claim you
  for a friend,
But look out, boys, he's easy for to
  bend!   (Chorus)

Oh, the merchant he's a dodger,
  Yes, a well-known dodger,
Oh, the merchant he's a dodger,
  Yes, and I'm a dodger, too.
He'll sell you the goods at double
  the price,
But when you go to pay him, you'll
  have to pay him twice!   (Chorus)

Oh, the farmer he's a dodger,
  Yes, a well-known dodger,
Oh, the farmer he's a dodger,
  Yes, and I'm a dodger, too.
He'll plow his cotton, he'll plow
  his corn,
But he won't make a living just as
  sure as you are born!   (Chorus)

Oh, the sheriff he's a dodger,
  Yes, a well-known dodger,
Oh, the sheriff he's a dodger,
  Yes, and I'm a dodger, too.
He'll act like a friend and a
  mighty fine man,
But, look out, boys, he'll put you
  in the can.   (Chorus)

Oh, the lover he's a dodger,
  Yes, a well-known dodger,
Oh, the lover he's a dodger,
  Yes, and I'm a dodger, too.
He'll hug you and kiss you and
  call you his bride,
But, look out, girls, he's telling
  you a lie!   (Chorus)

I Am a Girl
of Constant Sorrow

Words by Sarah Ogan
Music: Traditional

In 1932, Sarah Ogan, a young miner's wife in Harlan County, Kentucky, had to leave her home because most of her family was blacklisted from the mines for having led a strike. This song is a true document of her life and is but one of many she made up. The melody is from an old mountain ballad.

I am a girl of con-stant sor - row. I've seen trou - ble all my days. I bid fare - well to old Ken- tuck - y, the place where I was born and raised.

My mother, how I hated to leave her,
Mother dear, she now is dead.
But I had to go and leave her
So my children could have bread.

Perhaps, dear friends, you are a-
  wondering
What the miners eat and wear.
This question I will try to answer
For I am sure that it is fair.

For breakfast we had bulldog gravy,
For supper we had beans and bread.
The miners don't have any dinner,
And a tick of straw they call a bed.

Well, our clothes are always ragged,
And our feet are always bare.
And I know if there's a heaven
That we all are going there.

Well, we call this Hell on earth,
  friends;
I must tell you all goodbye.
Oh I know you all are hungry;
Oh, my darling friends, don't cry.

I'm A-Looking for a Home

This 1946 version of the old song, "The Boll Weevil," was originally made up by "The Priority Ramblers," union singers of Washington, D. C. The first and last verses were added by Bernie Bell, just discharged from the army. You can change around the words to make it fit your own home town.

Four long years in the ar-my, It nev-er was a home. Take me back to New York town and nev-er more I'll roam, I'm a-look-ing for a home, I'm a-look-ing for a home.

My first day in New York town,
I spent looking for a bed,
Searching all the avenues
For a place to lay my head.
   (Chorus after each verse)

One lady said she had a room,
I said, "Is that correct?"
"You can have it on one condition --
That the dog does not object."

I answered an advertisement,
I went down in a crowd,
The landlady, she made a speech:
"No dogs, no cats, no kids,
No chickens, no workingmen allowed."

The first time I saw my bedroom
It had just a bed and a chair,
The next time I saw my bedroom
There were five guys sleeping there.

I left my room for a minute
Just to get a glass of beer
When I got back there were four more men
Swinging on the chandelier.

If you should see anybody
Come round here looking for me,
I spend my days in Central Park
And my nights on the IRT.

Copyright 1946.

Mad As I Can Be

Words and music by Baldwin Hawes
Copyright 1946 by Baldwin Hawes

I'm as mad as I can be don't talk to me.
I'm so dog-gone mad that I can hard-ly see.
war is o-ver and the bat-tle's done, Stand here wond'rin' what we won.
Pri-ces up and the pay-scale's down, Ev'-ry-bo-dy broke in my home town, It's mean, it's bad, and it ain't a-ny fun when down in the Se-nate in Wash-ing-ton they're throw-ing out ev'-ry good thing we ev-er done.

I'm as mad as I can be -- don't speak to me.
I'm so doggone mad that I can hardly see.
Everybody's gotta have a job with pay,
And that's the problem till you're old and gray.
You can double-talk this and you can double-talk that,
But you can't get around that problem, Jack --
Honest pay for an honest chore,
And an honest dollar the corner store,
That's the job I hired my Senator for.

The Rankin Tree

Words and music by
Lee Hays and Walter Lowenfels
(c) 1946 by Lee Hays

Well, I had a farm // and on that farm // there

was a tree // and the name of the tree // it was the Rank-in Tree // It

grew so big // that it hid the sun // for miles a - round //

pois - oned ev'-ry-thing // in the ground // It poi-soned my po-ta-toes // it

poi-soned my squash // it mil-dewed all // of my Mon-day wash // It

killed my horse // killed my pig // In fact that tree // got too damn big // So I

got my lit - tle axe // and put it on the stone // and I turned stone // a-

round and a-round // and wet-ted the blade // till the edg-es shone // Then I

went to the tree // and one two three // I chopped it down // and I

laid it on the ground // and I chopped it up // for kind-ling wood // I

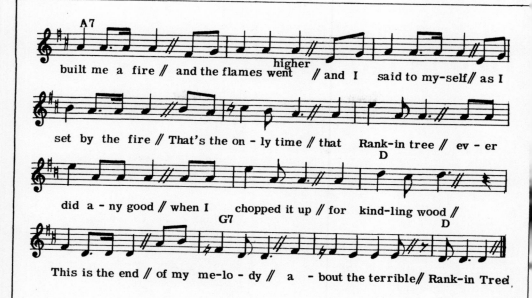

built me a fire // and the flames went *higher* // and I said to my-self // as I

set by the fire // That's the on - ly time // that Rank-in tree // ev - er

did a - ny good // when I chopped it up // for kind-ling wood //

This is the end // of my me-lo - dy // a - bout the terrible // Rank-in Tree.

The Scabs Crawl In

This is not a "performance song" but is one of the very best chants for a bunch of pickets to take up when they see some scabs sneaking in or out of the plant.

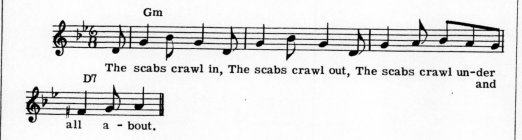

The scabs crawl in, The scabs crawl out, The scabs crawl un-der and

all a - bout.

They crawl by day, they crawl by night,
They crawl because they're afraid to
    fight.

They crawl in early, they crawl in late,
They crawl in under the factory gate.

This Song has no ending - Keep on Going!

United Nations
Make a Chain

This song is based on a traditional Negro spiritual. At least three song-writers have come up with United Nations versions of it in recent months. A special plenum of these writers was called and here's the song that was reported in by the majority.

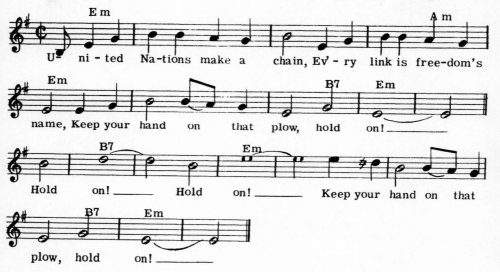

U-ni-ted Na-tions make a chain, Ev'-ry link is free-dom's name, Keep your hand on that plow, hold on! Hold on! Hold on! Keep your hand on that plow, hold on!

Now the war is over and done,
Let's keep the peace that we have won,
Keep your hand on the plow, hold on!

Freedom's name is mighty sweet,
Black and white are gonna meet,
Keep your hand on the plow, hold on!

Many men have fought and died,
So we could be here side by side,
Keep your hand on the plow, hold on!